# WHAT I LEARNED IN NARNIA

# WHAT I LEARNED
## *in* Narnia

### DOUGLAS WILSON

canonpress
Moscow, Idaho

*Also by Douglas Wilson*

Future Men

The Case for Classical Christian Education

Is Christianity Good for the World?
A Debate with Christopher Hitchens

Heaven Misplaced
Christ's Kingdom on Earth

Standing on the Promises
A Handbook for Biblical Childrearing

This book is dedicated to
KEITH AND GLADYS HUNT,
who introduced our family
to the world of Narnia
in 1958, when I was five.
Many, many thanks.

Published by Canon Press
P.O. Box 8729, Moscow, ID 83843
800–488–2034 | www.canonpress.com

Douglas Wilson, *What I Learned in Narnia*
Copyright © 2010 by Douglas Wilson

Scripture quotations are from the Authorized Version unless otherwise noted. Quotations from *The Chronicles of Narnia* are taken from the 1994 HarperCollins editions.

Cover and interior design by Laura Storm.
Cover photography by ANP.
Printed in the United States of America.

*Library of Congress Cataloging-in-Publication Data*

Wilson, Douglas, 1953-
   What I learned in Narnia / Douglas Wilson.
      p. cm.
   ISBN-13: 978-1-59128-079-8 (pbk.)
   ISBN-10: 1-59128-079-6 (pbk.)
   1. Lewis, C. S. (Clive Staples), 1898-1963. Chronicles of Narnia. 2. Christianity in literature. 3. Spirituality in literature. I. Title.
   PR6023.E926Z97 2010
   823'.912--dc22

                                        2010029748

11  12  13  14  15  16  17      10  9  8  7  6  5  4  3  2

# CONTENTS

*Acknowledgments*                                    9

*Introduction*                                       11


1. AUTHORITY                                         13

2. CONFESSION OF SIN                                 39

3. NOBILITY                                          63

4. SPIRITUAL DISCIPLINES                             85

5. LOVE OF STORY                                     109

6. THOROUGH GRACE                                    129

7. LOVE FOR ASLAN, LOVE FOR GOD                      145

# Acknowledgments

I WOULD LIKE to begin by thanking Lucy Jones and the team at Canon Press for their great idea of making a book out of these talks that I gave a few years ago to some of the children in our church. A special thanks should also be extended to Jared Miller for his wonderful work in taking my outlines and the recordings of the talks and coming up with such a fine mash-up. As I read through the results of his labors, my thought was, "Surely I cannot have spoken this smoothly." Which, I can assure you, I had not.

Thanks also go to my parents who saw to it that my brothers and sister and I grew up marinating in the Narnia stories. It seems in retrospect that I was brought up as a Narnian. And in watching our crazy world go by, I am tempted to wonder why I don't need a green card to live here.

And of course, I should thank C. S. Lewis, a man who has had a greater influence on me than all the other authors I have ever read combined. I often find Lewis at the end of every train of thought, near the root of every tree. Debts are not discharged simply by acknowledging them, but gratitude, however feebly expressed, must still be expressed. I am profoundly grateful.

# INTRODUCTION

I WOULD LIKE to introduce this small book by pleading with the reader to put it down immediately if he has not yet read the Narnia stories. This is the kind of book that would be best read after the reader is thoroughly acquainted with Puddleglum, and with Tirian, and with Digory, Lucy, Caspian, Trumpkin, and of course, Aslan. So this is not intended to be an introduction to Narnia at all, but is rather more like a conversation between good friends about some other good friends, talking about what a good time we all had and why. But in order to have that conversation, we have to have the good time first.

If the Narnia stories are simply read, and enjoyed, and repeatedly read, and repeatedly enjoyed, then the things I am talking about in this book will be part of the reader's "bone knowledge." I have no desire to present this book as though I want the reader to squeeze any moral out of these stories before they have ever had the pleasure of settling down on a rainy afternoon to enjoy one of them. A rush to moralize has wrecked many a good story, and I don't want to do that here. But at the same time, good stories are the sorts of stories you do learn from—as C. S. Lewis knew full well. And if we learn from his wonderful stories, we should be able to discuss it.

By the title of the book, *What I Learned in Narnia,* I don't mean to indicate that these seven lessons were all I learned there. A much thicker book than this could be written if we were to discuss all the things contained in the world of Narnia—whether they were other things learned, or lessons I have not yet learned. Michael Ward's wonderful book, *Planet Narnia,* comes to mind—Ward pointed out for me a number of things I had learned without knowing anything at all about it. All that said, these basic truths were at the center of how the Lord used these stories in my life. It is my hope that you will be able to say the same.

# CHAPTER 1

# AUTHORITY

AUTHORITY IS INESCAPABLE. This means that people can use authority rightly or wrongly, but we cannot avoid altogether having people in positions of authority. In the same way, people can *submit* to authority rightly or wrongly (or to the right or wrong authority), but they will always be submitting to some kind of authority. Authority is something that God built into the world, and by right of creation He is the ultimate authority in it. But since humanity is sinful, we have many ways of either misusing authority or attempting to deny it altogether.

Before we see how Lewis handles the theme of authority in the Narnia series, let me tell a brief childhood story that illustrates fallen humanity's basic response to authority. One Saturday morning when I was about ten years old, I was for some reason having a great day—just feeling good about myself, the human race, and the world in general. As I was lying on the living room floor reading the comics, and filled with nothing but the milk of human kindness, I soon found myself thinking, "When I'm done with the comics, I'm going to surprise my mom by cleaning up the basement." But just when I was pondering this (and feeling really good about myself), my mother walked in and said, "Doug, I'd like you to go downstairs and clean the basement."

And just like that, she had wrecked everything. The milk of human kindness miraculously drained away, and in its place was a little black rain cloud of rebellious mutterings. Now think about this for a moment—*why* did her command wreck my day? I was going to clean the basement anyway, so she was not interrupting any special plans I had made. What was the big deal? Just this: If I had done it by myself I would not have been under any authority, and I would have gotten all sorts of brownie points for doing it. But after she had told me to do it, I would merely be obedient by doing it. And it was no fun being obedient; I wanted to be a *volunteer*. I was kicking against the very fact of being under authority.

Now in discussing the theme of authority in the Narnia books, I want to divide the topic into two basic sections: characters who have twisted attitudes toward authority, and those who have righteous attitudes toward it.

# False Authority

The Narnian chronicles contain many different characters who try to abuse authority in many different ways. But in the end, they all have one common thread. The root of all their problems is selfishness and grasping—the opposite of the biblical commands for leaders to be sacrificial and giving.

## Miraz, *Prince Caspian*

In *Prince Caspian*, Miraz is a usurper. Before the narrative begins, we find out that he had killed Prince Caspian's father, his own brother, in order to take power. Caspian knows nothing of this, having been very young when his father was killed. So as long as Miraz doesn't have a son of his own, he is happy to raise Caspian and allow him to be the next king after him. But when his wife, Queen Prunaprismia (a wonderfully named woman) gives birth to a baby boy, Miraz decides to kill Caspian so his own son can succeed him. With the help of Doctor Cornelius, Caspian escapes and finally learns that Miraz is not the lawful king.

Now Lewis makes an interesting historical reference here: "When he [Miraz] first began to rule he did not even pretend to be king. He called himself Lord Protector" (59). If you remember your history, you might recall that in seventeenth-century England, there was a war between Parliament (led by Oliver Cromwell) and King Charles I. The king lost the war and was beheaded. Cromwell then took over and called himself *Lord Protector* instead of *King*. Now Miraz begins by calling himself Lord Protector, but later shows his true colors when he gets his followers to declare him king—essentially admitting that he has been the acting king all along and that he never had any intention of "protecting" Caspian's rightful claim to the throne. Not only does his selfishness and grasping drive him to murder, he also spins his words deceitfully to hide it. His "authority" is entirely false—he is nothing but a murderer and a usurper.

## EUSTACE SCRUBB,
### *The Voyage of the Dawn Treader*
In *The Voyage of the Dawn Treader,* the Scrubb family portrays another kind of abuse of authority quite different from the usurpation of Miraz and somewhat more trivial and silly in comparison. In a brief side comment, Lewis writes: "[Eustace] didn't call his father and mother Father and Mother, but Harold and Alberta" (3). In this

case, Eustace's parents are not grasping after authority; rather, they are throwing away the rightful authority they have as parents, making themselves peers of their child. To describe what is going on in this passage better, I'm going to use a big word for a simple idea: *egalitarianism*. Egalitarianism is the view that everything in society should be leveled—everyone should be exactly equal. Egalitarians believe that men and women, parents and children, bosses and employees, and everyone else are (or at least should be) at the same level in society. In other words, they have a problem with structures of authority. And what C. S. Lewis is making fun of in this passage is that type of thinking that wants to reject all authority—including that of parents—which is why Eustace talks to them like they are his peers rather than respecting their role as parents who are in authority over him.

## JADIS, *The Magician's Nephew*

In *The Magician's Nephew*, Lewis contrasts two very different magicians with a common flaw: their abuse of a false authority. On the one hand we have Jadis, a sorceress and the last empress of Charn (who becomes the White Witch later in *The Lion, the Witch and the Wardrobe*). On the other hand we have Digory's Uncle Andrew, who believes himself to be a great magician but really does not understand the forces he is dealing with.

But Jadis and Uncle Andrew are both magicians. And in this book we see that Jadis and Uncle Andrew both believe they are "above the rules." They both believe rules are only for ordinary, common people. In this way, they try to put themselves above all authority but their own. They do not want anybody telling them what to do and they do not want any rules telling them what to do. The problem with this, of course, is that you should never trust people who have strong views of authority when talking about people *under* them, but have very weak views of authority when talking about people *over* them. Whenever you encounter someone like that, you need to run in the other direction as fast and as far as you can—that person is going to abuse any authority they can get. One of the best things C. S. Lewis teaches us is that true authority can only be exercised by leaders who delight in submitting to authority themselves.

Jadis and Uncle Andrew do not do this at all. At one point Jadis says,

> "I had forgotten that you are only a common boy. How should you understand reasons of State? You should learn, child, that what would be wrong for you, or any of the common people, is not wrong for a great Queen such as I. The weight of the world is on our shoulders. We must be freed from all rules. Ours is a high and lonely destiny." (68)

So not only is she claiming to be above the rules, she also wants Digory to feel sorry for her because of it. "Ours is a high and lonely destiny"—not only does she demand obedience, she expects pity as well! The ironic twist in this passage is how it reveals that her noble-sounding act is nothing but common selfishness. When she makes this statement, Digory suddenly remembers that Uncle Andrew had used exactly the same words earlier: "Ours is a high and lonely destiny, my boy." But, Digory thinks to himself, "they sounded much grander when Queen Jadis said them; perhaps because Uncle Andrew was not seven feet tall and dazzlingly beautiful" (68). What Lewis is saying is that no matter who you are—a seedy old man pretending to be a magician, or a beautiful seven-foot-tall queen—this "high and lonely destiny" business is just a thin excuse for selfish ambition at the expense of others.

## AHOSHTA, *The Horse and His Boy*

In *The Horse and His Boy* Lewis describes a very different type of bad authority from that of Jadis, but no less ugly. Recall that Aravis, the heroine of the story, runs away from her father's house when she finds out that her father is going to force her into marrying a man named Ahoshta. Some time later in the story, we find out what kind of man this Ahoshta is. Lasaraleen, Aravis's old friend, is scolding her for running away from the marriage when she says, "My husband says [Ahoshta] is beginning to be one of the greatest men in Calormen" (100).

But when we finally get to see this "great man," what is he like? He is groveling on the carpet in front of his master, the Tisroc, and Rabadash the prince is kicking him in the rear end for saying the wrong things. So, on the one hand he is "one of the greatest men in Calormen," but on the other he is a greasy, flattering, manipulating weasel. The authority that he wields—and he does wield real authority in Calormen—springs not from being a wise, strong man with real qualities of character, but from groveling, allowing himself to be abused, and playing the system through flattery. This is false authority as well as false submission. True submission never grovels, and true authority never accepts flattery.

## SHIFT THE MANIPULATOR, *The Last Battle*

*The Last Battle* is many people's least favorite book in the Narnian Chronicles, and while I can understand their objections, I think it has a lot going for it. Shift, the aptly-named ape, is one of the best-drawn characters in all the

Narnia stories, and he provides yet another example of misused authority.

Shift manipulates to get his way. He exercises authority by lies and trickery, all the while convincing his victims that he is only looking out for their best interests. For example, let's look at how Shift manipulates his so-called friend, Puzzle the donkey.

> "Really, Puzzle," said Shift, "I didn't think you'd ever say a thing like that. I didn't think it of you, really."
> "Why, what have I said wrong?" said the Ass, speaking in rather a humble voice, for he saw that Shift was very deeply offended. (4)

Now what is Shift doing in this passage by acting offended? He is manipulating Puzzle by creating false guilt. Have you ever seen someone moping around, waiting for others to feel sorry for him? (Maybe you have even done this yourself.) Perhaps this type of person wants pity, or perhaps they want to instill a false sense of guilt in someone, but the goal is always the same—somehow they want to get their way. There is something they want—maybe they just want to feel some kind of power over others—and they manipulate others' feelings in order to get it.

That is just what Shift is doing here. He acts deeply offended because he knows that Puzzle has a tender heart, and he knows that this is one way to get Puzzle to do what he wants. Shift has completely turned the golden rule upside-down. Instead of "I will treat you as I want you to treat me," Shift says, "Why don't you treat me as I treat you?" (9). The difference being that Shift *really* means, "Why don't you treat me the way I *say* I treat you (not how I actually treat you). And as long as I can convince you that I am acting in your best interests instead of my own, I will get away with it."

When Shift succeeds at getting into power, his manipulations only get amplified as his audience grows. First of all, he dresses up, which is Lewis's way of highlighting Shift's deceitfulness. "The ape was of course Shift himself, but he looked ten times uglier than when he lived by cauldron pool, for he was now dressed up" (32). Lewis is saying that if you put royal robes on an ape, you don't have a king— you just have an ape in robes. In the same way, Shift dresses up his words to seem slick and sophisticated on the surface, but they are still nothing but ugly, grasping selfishness underneath. And not only that, but they are ten times worse than if he had not tried to cover them up that way.

But the real evil of Shift's authority is how he manipulates the Narnians' belief in Aslan to benefit himself. At one point he says, "Attend to me! I want—I mean *Aslan* wants—some more nuts" (33). This is one of the oldest tricks in the book for sinful leaders: once you get into power, take whatever you can from the people, but all in the name of a higher good. This higher good may be God, or patriotism, or humanistic brotherhood, or democracy, but what all such power-abusers really want is more power for themselves. Unlike Shift, they usually remember to say "the greater good of society requires this" instead of "*I* want this," but that does not make it any less ridiculous than saying, "Aslan wants more nuts."

## The Dwarfs, *The Last Battle*

The final misuse of authority we will cover in this chapter is also from *The Last Battle*. Recall that near the end of the book, Iterion and the others liberate the dwarfs who have been enslaved and are being taken off to the Tisroc's mines. But how do the dwarfs respond to this liberation? You would think they would express gratitude and loyalty to their savior, but they don't. They say, "We're going to look after ourselves from now on and touch our caps to nobody" (83). Now "touch our caps" is a sign of respect and deference to someone, a way of showing honor to authority. The dwarfs think that because they were en-slaved once, all authorities must be slave-masters. So they are determined to shake off all authority. Their rallying cry becomes, "The dwarfs are for the dwarfs." They react against one bad authority by refusing to acknowledge any authority at all.

# True Authority

All these characters we have discussed so far—Miraz, Jadis, Ahoshta, Shift, the dwarfs—either get their authority in wrongful, conniving ways, or selfishly abuse the authority they already have, or (most commonly) both. They are constantly asking themselves, "How much can I get? How much can I take?" Despite all the superficial differences among these characters, this is the one thing they all share. And this sort of pride and selfishness is, we might say, the root of nearly all other kinds of sin; like Adam and Eve in the Garden, we believe *we* are right and God (not to mention everyone else) is wrong. It also comes naturally to fallen human beings. Nobody has to teach kids how to grab a toy or bonk somebody else on the head; go into any nursery and you will see it happening within minutes. They are born knowing how to grab and how to want things for themselves. This is the basic problem that Jesus came to deal with, and it can be seen most clearly in how authority is wrongfully gotten and used.

We now turn to the Narnian characters who create a righteous contrast to all these bad examples of authority. And just as in our world we would begin this discussion with the work of Jesus, in the context of Narnia we begin with Aslan.

But before we begin, I need to say something about the connection between Aslan and Jesus. C. S. Lewis was very adamant in saying that the Narnia books are not an *allegory.* An allegory is a book like *Pilgrim's Progress,* in which the characters and their actions have a one-to-one correspondence to another layer of meaning. Think of an allegory as a two-story building—the first story is the actual narrative and characters, while the second story is the set of abstract ideas they represent. In *Pilgrim's Progress* the hero starts out with a heavy burden strapped to his back—this is the "first story" thing. In the "second story" of meaning, this burden represents his sins. Later in the story, the hero meets a giant who represents the sin of despair, and so on. One thing on the first story exactly represents one other thing on the second story, and the author typically makes the meanings clear.

Now C. S. Lewis maintained that the Narnian Chronicles were *not* like this. There is not a one-to-one correspondence between a character, object, or event in Narnia and some abstraction that Lewis wanted to teach us about. Instead, Lewis called these books "a great supposal." Suppose there were another world like Narnia and suppose that God entered into that world in a way similar to the way he entered into our world—what would that be like? So, in general the inhabitants of Narnia do not have single, allegorical meanings. But Aslan obviously does fill the place of Jesus in this "great supposal." He once tells the children that when they get back to England they will know him there by "another name." At the end of *The Voyage of the Dawn Treader* we see a vision of him as a lamb, the Christian symbol of Jesus. In *The Last Battle,* when everything converges at a final judgment, it is again very clear that Aslan is Christ the Judge.

Just as in our world all true authority flows from Jesus Christ, so also in Narnia all true authority flows from Aslan. Aslan sets the pattern of true authority that his followers imitate, and the basic foundation of this authority, in direct contrast to the bad characters we have been reading about, is one of *sacrifice* and *giving*.

## True Authority is Sacrificial

In our natural frame of mind, we sinful humans tend to think that if you grab, you gain, and if you sacrifice, you lose. But what the Bible teaches, and what C. S. Lewis writes into the Narnia books everywhere, is exactly the opposite: if you grab, you lose, but if you give, you get. Authority flows to the person who sacrifices himself in order to give to others, but the person who tries to force authority away from others only ends up losing it. Imagine for a moment that you are a third-grade kid, and a fourth-grader walks up to you and says, "I want you to respect me and do everything I say, because I'm in the fourth grade." The chances are pretty good that you would not do anything of the sort after hearing that, even if you might have before. Why? Because when people *demand* respect and authority, it runs away from them. But when they give themselves up for others, authority flows to them. You grab, you lose; you give, you gain.

Now suppose you walk into the kitchen the same time as your brother or sister, and you both reach for the plate with one cookie on it. You know the right thing to do is to give it up. But are you giving it up only in order to *get*? In other words, you might be thinking "Wait! Are you telling me that if I let her take the cookie now, then I get a cookie later?" Maybe you are hoping your mother will see your great act of kindness and bake you a dozen more on the spot. But no—in this case, your sister will get the cookie and you will not. That sort of wooden interpretation is not the kind of giving-to-get that I am talking about here. And it is wrong because its expectations are far too *low*. The biblical lesson is that a giving pattern of life is going to yield many, many blessings that are much greater than all the small things you have given up.

God provides a clear example of this in Genesis 13. Abraham and Lot were both so wealthy in flocks and herds that "the land was not able to bear them" and fights broke out amongst their servants. So Abraham suggests that they part ways, and sacrificing his own preference, he tells Lot that he can have the first choice: "Is not the whole land before thee? Separate thyself, I pray thee, from me: if thou wilt take the left hand, then I will go to the right; or if thou depart to the right hand, then I will go to the left" (v. 9). Lot's response to this is not gratitude, but greed; he chooses the obviously better land that is lush and green (vv. 10–11). But it turns out that this land is right next to Sodom and Gomorrah, which are later destroyed by fire from heaven. So Lot, through his selfish grasping, got the better deal in the short term but was ruined in the long term. Abraham, meanwhile, took what appeared to be the worse option at first, but God blessed him much more richly in the end.

This principle comes to life again and again in the Narnia stories. What happens to Miraz? When he grabs for power, he loses it. What happens to Jadis? Her empire in Charn is destroyed and she makes her way into Narnia, where after a one hundred-year reign she is finally defeated and killed. What happens to Shift? He is thrown through the stable door and the evil Calormene god Tash eats him— one peck and he is gone. In the same story, the dwarfs are thrown through the stable door but they are blinded to the glorious place that is there—they are in heaven but they make it a hell for themselves. Again and again, good things run away from people who *grab*, and good things (including authority) flow to people who *give*.

Aslan is, of course, the chief example and pattern of this principle, and he is just like Jesus in this respect. But the witch in *The Lion, the Witch and the Wardrobe* only understands the grabbing kind of authority—if you want something, you take it. She does not understand Aslan's kind of authority at all. What does she think when Aslan comes to negotiate Edmund's release? Remember that Edmund had betrayed his brother and sisters, and because of that, even though he had been rescued from the witch, she has a lawful claim on him because he is a traitor. Aslan does not dispute the claim. Instead, he does something that is shocking and incomprehensible to all those who, like the witch, only understand the grasping kind of authority: He agrees to give himself in exchange for Edmund. This is because Aslan knows that the way to authority is through sacrifice. Even so, when Aslan fulfills his part of the agreement, it is very difficult for him. Just understanding the principle of sacrifice does not automatically make that sacrifice easy. When he goes to his death, he is so sorrowful that he allows Lucy and Susan to accompany him part way and provide some comfort and companionship.

When the witch sees Aslan coming, she believes she has triumphed. "'The fool!' she cried, 'The fool has come. Bind him fast'" (151). All she understands is what Aslan calls the "deep magic," which allows a traitor to be freed if another chooses to die in his place.

But after Aslan comes back to life, he explains the witch's mistake: "'It means,' said Aslan, 'That though the witch knew the deep magic, there is a magic deeper still which she did not know'" (163). The deeper magic is that love and sacrifice conquer hate and greed. Love and sacrifice create true, ultimate authority. So it is not just that Aslan died for Edmund as the perfect, substitutionary sacrifice for a traitor, thus saving him—though of course he did die in Edmund's place and he did save him. There is more to it: After his death and resurrection, Aslan gains true authority. He had authority before, but after this it grows and changes in a glorious way.

But sinful people cannot understand this "deep magic." You can explain it, read it from the Bible, draw it on a blackboard, and shout it at the top of your lungs, but a sinful heart cannot know this principle: *if you give, you get.* They just cannot get it into their heads—or rather, into their *hearts.* For they do not have an intellectual problem; they have a spiritual problem.

So Aslan's authority springs from love and sacrifice. But this does not mean that his world is all sunshine and rainbows. Frequently the people whom he loves and saves find it to be very unpleasant at the time—Edmund certainly does. And his enemies ultimately experience his judgment, not his love. Earlier in the book one of the children asks, "Is Aslan safe?" To which Mr. Beaver replies,

> "Safe? Don't you hear what Mrs. Beaver tells you? Who said anything about safe? Of course he isn't safe. But he's good. He's the king, I tell you." (80)

He is good, but his kind of goodness is often unsettling and frightening—unsettling to Edmund and frightening to the witch.

## True Authority is Humble

All the villains mentioned so far—Miraz, Jadis, Uncle Andrew, Shift, and even Ahoshta, whose groveling is not anything like true humility—are proud and self-absorbed, which goes hand-in-hand with their false authority. But Aslan is the pattern of true, sacrificial authority, and when he bestows this kind of authority on his servants, true humility comes along with it. Of course none of them are perfect—they have remaining sins and flaws—but they consistently exercise authority with true humility.

Consider the test of kingship that Aslan gives to Caspian.

> "Welcome, Prince," said Aslan. "Do you feel yourself sufficient to take up the Kingship of Narnia?"
>
> "I—I don't think I do, Sir," said Caspian. "I'm only a kid."
>
> "Good," said Aslan. "If you had felt yourself sufficient, it would have been a proof that you were not." (206)

Aslan's test is a test of humility. If Caspian had said something along the lines of, "Yeah, I'm ready—I've been ready for years but Miraz kept me from having it," then it would have been obvious that Caspian was just another Miraz—proud, selfish, and grasping. But Caspian realizes the true nature of authority, which involves great personal sacrifice, and this realization produces humility. He admits he does not feel ready to take on such a burden, and paradoxically, that means he *is* ready.

I have had the opportunity to officiate at many weddings over the years, and this is one question that I think should be asked of every bridegroom at some point before the final vows: "Are you ready for this?" A good, honest answer, from a man who fully understands what he is getting into, should be "No!" And this, of course, means that he is well on his way to being ready.

Aslan gives a similar test in *The Magician's Nephew* when he makes a London cabby the first king of Narnia. At first the cabby resists, saying he's not the right chap for the job and that he never had much "eddycation."

But Aslan asks him a series of questions about whether he could farm, rule the talking creatures of Narnia fairly, raise children to do the same, not play favorites, and in battle be "the first in the charge and the last in the retreat" (151–152). In the end, Aslan pronounces him ready.

Now clearly this is not a simplistic rule that we can apply willy-nilly to all aspects of life. Just because a fourth grader does not feel ready for twelfth grade does not mean that he is, on some deeper level, *actually* ready for twelfth grade. He really is not ready, regardless of how he feels. But when someone is, in any part of their life, about to move on to the next level—whether it is another level of schooling, taking up a new sport, or learning a new subject, or moving out on one's own, or getting married, or having children, or becoming a leader of others—then this test can apply, especially when people around you, people whom you respect, think that you should take that step. And if, on such an occasion, you find yourself honestly thinking "I don't know if I can do this," then that is a good sign. God has put you there for a reason. He wants you to take up the challenge, and He will give you the ability to do it.

In *The Horse and His Boy,* when Shasta (now known by his birth name, Cor) learns that he is to be the king of Archenland, he does not like the idea at all. And when Corin, his younger twin brother who would have been king if Cor had not turned up, discovers that he gets to be a prince instead of a king for the rest of his life, he is overjoyed. Now at first this does not make sense to us. Why isn't Cor gloating about being king, and why is Corin not envious and bitter? The answer is that at heart, they are both servants of Aslan and as such they have humble hearts. But the main thing in this passage is that Cor does not at all grasp after the kingship:

"But I don't want it," said Cor. "I'd far rather—"

[King Lune replied,] "'Tis no question what thou wantest, Cor, nor I either. 'Tis in the course of the law. ... The king's under the law, for it's the law makes him king. Hast no more power to start away from thy crown than any sentry from his post. . . .

"For this is what it means to be king: to be first in every desperate attack and last in every desperate retreat, and when there's hunger in the land (as must be now and then in bad years) to wear finer clothes and laugh louder over a scantier meal than any man in your land." (222–223)

Being king is not about sitting in a fine castle and ordering everyone to do your every bidding. That is the Tisroc's idea of leadership, but not the Narnian or Archenlander view at all. The key point in this passage is that the king is the servant of law; the king is not above the law. And that applies before he even becomes king—if the law calls him to be king, he must not refuse. Just as a soldier sent off to guard duty has no right to abandon his post, so the one chosen to be king has no right to abandon his kingship. If you run away from your duty, you become a deserter.

King Lune's speech also shows that it is the king's responsibility to "take the hit" for his people, whatever the "hit" might be. Authority should not serve to cushion the king from the world; rather, it is the king who should bear the brunt of every blow. It is the same not just for kings and presidents and congressmen and other political leaders, but also for anyone who has authority—a husband for his wife, a father for his children, an elder or pastor for his congregation. If you are assigned a leadership role by God, then you step forward and you take up a bigger burden than anyone else. You ought not to say, "Well, now that I'm in charge, I'm going to order people around so that I can relax." That is the opposite of true, humble authority.

## Authority and Obedience

So far we have talked about true and false authority in the context of the people who are in positions of authority. But what about those who are under authority? What is the right and wrong way to *respond* to the authority of others?

My favorite example of this in the Narnia stories is a short speech by Trumpkin the dwarf in *Prince Caspian*. At this point in the story, the army of Caspian and the Old Narnians is in a standoff with Miraz's army, besieged at the great mound called Aslan's How, and the Old Narnians are getting the worst of it. As they discuss plans for their final stand against Miraz, Caspian and his advisers decide to use the horn of Queen Susan which, when blown by someone in a desperate situation, will magically summon help. According to Doctor Cornelius it will be either Aslan or "Peter the High King and his mighty consorts down from the high past" (96). Now Trumpkin hates Miraz and is loyal to Caspian, but he does not believe in Aslan or the other ancient legends, including the magic horn—he thinks of himself as a practical fellow, and it is all just "eggs and moonshine" to him (96). But he is outnumbered and so submits to the council's decision, asking them only to not tell the troops what they are doing, so as not to raise false hopes.

Then Doctor Cornelius tells the council that the help will come either to their camp, or to the Lantern Waste (where the four children first appeared in Narnia), or in the ruins of Cair Paravel. So they must send messengers to the two other places to find out if the horn brought help. Again, Trumpkin is skeptical: "The first result of all this foolery is not to bring us help but to lose us two fighters" (97). Now Trumpkin has twice stated his complete disagreement with the council, but then he does a surprising thing—he volunteers to be one of the two messengers. His attitude takes even Caspian by surprise.

> "But I thought you didn't believe in the horn, Trumpkin," said Caspian.
> "No more I do, your majesty. But what's that got to do with it? I might as well die in a wild goose chase as die here. You are my King. I know the difference between giving advice and taking orders. You've had my advice, and now it's the time for orders." (98)

This is a very important lesson on authority. Regardless of his complete disagreement with Caspian and the council's decision, Trumpkin remains loyal to them and respectfully submits to their authority. There is a clear difference between *advice* and *orders*. It is the duty of everyone under authority to give their advice when asked, just as it is the duty of those in authority to carefully consider the advice of those below them. But at some point a decision must be made, and that is when those under authority need to be ready for orders. There is a time for advice, but when the time comes for obedience, life is very simple: obey. The lesson may be simple, but that does not mean the application of it is easy. This kind of obedience should not involve grumbling and foot-dragging. Obedience should be wholehearted whether you think the task is a good idea or not.

Many people today, in the grip of egalitarianism and individualism, react violently against this idea. The objection goes something like this: "How can you teach such mindless obedience? Do you want people to act like brainwashed cult members? People should be individuals who think for themselves!" Of course, this objection is a very bad caricature of what we are talking about here, and another passage in *Prince Caspian* answers it by showing that even true loyalty like Trumpkin's has limits. Earlier in the story, Nikabrik and his friends suggested to Caspian that they call for aid from the "dark" creatures of Old Narnia—hags, ogres, werewolves, and even (later on, in a different passage) the spirit of the White Witch herself. Trufflehunter the faithful badger quickly objects:

> "We should not have Aslan for friend if we brought in *that* rabble," said Trufflehunter as they came away from the cave of the Black Dwarfs.
> "Oh, Aslan!" said Trumpkin, cheerily but contemptuously. "What matters more is that you wouldn't have me." (77)

In other words, Trumpkin is threatening to quit the army because he has a standard of right and wrong that is above Caspian. If Caspian tells him to go on a risky, long-shot mission, Trumpkin will cheerfully obey even if he thinks the mission is a bad idea, and he will do his duty as fully and valiantly as he can. But if Caspian orders him to do something that is not just a bad idea, but also *morally wrong*—like welcoming evil creatures into their army and fighting alongside them—then Trumpkin will refuse to obey.

And you should note that he has a good deal of credibility when he says this, because he is not refusing simply because he does not feel like obeying at the moment. On the contrary, we later on see him cheerfully obey orders that he personally disagrees with. Trumpkin is not at all a mindless slave who will obey Caspian's every whim. He is an individual with a high standard of integrity, and he submits to Caspian's legitimate authority while knowing that it can cross a certain line and become illegitimate. The key is the common standard of right and wrong that is above them both.

In the same way, we know that as Christians we are called to obey the civil government. We are to pay our taxes and follow the laws of the land, even though we might personally disagree with some of them. But this does not mean that the government can tell us to do anything it pleases. If politicians tell us that we must disobey God and, in Narnian terms, have fellowship with hags and ogres, then we must tell them *no*. We are to serve God rather than men in those cases where men tell us to do something that God clearly forbids, or not to do something that God clearly commands (Acts 4:18–19). However, our protests will carry a great deal more weight if we have already demonstrated that we are willing to obey the civil authorities on other issues, even when it pinches our personal convenience.

*The Silver Chair* provides another example of loyalty in someone who is under authority. Near the beginning of the book, Eustace and Jill are secretly flown to a "parliament" of owls in the middle of the night. The owls want to discuss how to help them find the lost prince Rilian and they are doing so without the knowledge of Caspian's government (recall that Caspian had just sailed away, and Trumpkin the dwarf was looking after things in his place). Eustace has been away from Narnia for several decades and is not quite sure what kind of gathering it is and whose side they are on, especially because of the odd circumstances of the meeting. He does not know the ins and outs of Narnian politics, but he knows where he stands, and his first words are a great testament to his character:

"And what I want to say is this, that I'm the King's man; and if this parliament of owls is any sort of plot against the King, I'm having nothing to do with it." (53–54)

Eustace is quite willing to follow the advice of the owls, but he knows where his real loyalties are and he is willing to stand against the owls if they contradict those loyalties. Now, as it turns out, the owls are all quite harmless and all loyal to the king. They merely give their help in secret because the king had banned all Narnians from going on quests for the prince, since no one who had gone had ever come back. So Eustace had nothing to be concerned about, but it is still important that his first thought was how to preserve his loyalty to Caspian.

The last example I want to give in this chapter is also from *The Silver Chair*. Recall that Aslan gives Jill and Eustace a series of signs to follow in order to help them on their quest to find the lost prince. Through their squabbling and lack of faith and other failings, they "muff" all the first signs, and only by the goodness of Aslan do they get back on track and finally arrive at the place, deep underneath the ruined city of the giants, where they were to find the prince. Here they meet a knight who says he serves a great Lady. He seems good-hearted but also a bit empty-headed, as if there is something not quite right with his mind. He tells them he is under an enchantment which makes him go into a fit of violent madness at the same time every evening, so he has to be strapped into a silver chair so that he does not hurt anyone. Just to be sure, he makes the children and Puddleglum swear that they will not release him from the chair, no matter what he says or how much he begs them to.

Now the final sign Aslan had given Jill was that the lost prince would be the first person in all their journeying who would ask them to do something in the name of Aslan.

And as the knight is tied to the silver chair in his fit of madness, he finally gives them that very sign:

> "Once and for all," said the prisoner, "I adjure you
> to set me free. By all fears and all loves, by the bright
> skies of Overland, by the great Lion, by Aslan himself,
> I charge you [to release me]."
> "Oh," said the three travelers as though they'd been
> hurt. "It's the sign," said Puddleglum. "It was the *words*
> of the sign," said Scrubb more cautiously. "Oh what *are*
> we to do?" said Jill. (166)

For the knight is, of course, the lost Prince Rilian himself, and although he is continually under an enchantment, this "fit"—as his enchanted self calls it—is actually the one hour of the day that he is in his right mind. But Eustace and Jill and Puddleglum do not know this. They still think he is a raving lunatic, and when he speaks the final sign it forces them to make a decision. Should they obey the sign, release him, and risk getting slashed to pieces by a madman, or should they leave him tied up and assume that his calling on the name of Aslan was all just a mistake or coincidence?

> "On the other hand, what had been the use of learning
> the signs if they weren't going to obey them? . . .
> "Do you mean you think everything will come right
> if we do untie him?" said Scrubb.
> "I don't know about that," said Puddleglum. "You see,
> Aslan didn't tell [Jill] what would happen. He only told
> her what to do." (167)

Despite their confusion and uncertainty, the choice is really very simple. It is a matter of authority and obedience. Aslan himself gave them the signs, but he did not tell them that obeying them would keep them safe. They can believe and obey—regardless of the consequences—or they can not believe and not obey. In the end, they make the right choice, even if it means possibly being killed by a lunatic. Of course, nothing of the sort happens—instead, by freeing Rilian from the chair they break his enchantment and set the story on the path to a happy ending. But they did not know that when they made the decision to cut him loose. Their faith and loyalty to Aslan came first, even if it meant sacrificing themselves.

# Conclusion

Nearly every villain in the Narnia stories is a selfish grasper of some sort. They all try to clutch at authority, demand it from others, and force it upon themselves. In the end, however, authority flees far from them.

On the opposite side is the sacrificial authority of Aslan, who sets a pattern for all his followers by giving himself away. The world, like Jadis the White Witch, thinks this idea is completely foolish, but that is because it does not understand the "deeper magic" at work.

All the great heroes of Narnia follow this pattern—from Caspian to Cor and King Lune—and as they sacrifice themselves to be great leaders, they attract followers like Trumpkin who will sacrifice themselves to follow them. There is a certain authority in leading and a certain authority in following, but both share the same quality of *self-sacrifice*. Authority and submission are inescapable, but in the context of self-giving, they are liberating.

By learning this lesson and applying it deep down in your bones, you will always know the right thing to do. But without it, the world is a very dark and confusing place. The more you look at the world, the more you listen to what people on TV say, or maybe even what some of your friends say, the easier it is to get muddled in your thinking. "What does it all mean? Whom should I follow? What authorities should I be submitting to? My friends all say such-and-such is cool, but I know my parents and teachers would not think much of it."

At moments like these what you really need is the good, pungent smell of burnt Marsh-wiggle. Remember how Puddleglum became the hero of *The Silver Chair* when he stomped on the witch's fire that was confusing his companions' minds and making them doubt that Aslan or the whole world above ground ever existed?

> Suppose we *have* only dreamed, or made up, all those things—trees and grass and sun and moon and stars and Aslan himself. . . . Suppose this black pit of a kingdom of yours *is* the only world. Well, it strikes me as a pretty poor one. . . . I'm going to live as like a Narnian as I can even if there isn't any Narnia. (182)

Christians today desperately need this kind of faithfulness. When you are confused by the world's way of thinking, you need to be the Puddleglum who will just be obedient and stomp on the enchanted fire that is drugging your mind and your soul.

True authority and submission is one of the great lessons of Narnia—not only how to rule without being a tyrant, but also how to *obey* without being a mindless follower or a slave. If you refuse to obey at all—if you grab for that authority for yourself and say, "I'm not obeying anyone but myself; I'm going to have that authority," then you actually become a slave. But when you give it up, obey the authorities God has given you, and obey God Himself, He sets you free.

# CHAPTER 2

# CONFESSION OF SIN

BY NOW, HAVING read the title of this chapter, you are probably wondering why I chose confession of sin as one of the seven great themes I found in Narnia. But once you start looking for it, it is amazing how much the subject turns up in the stories—it plays an important role in all the books.

Another reason I chose the theme of confession is that it is one subject pastors can never talk too much about. My father was a preacher who spoke at various conferences all over the country, and one of his favorite talks was on exactly this subject, so you can imagine I grew up hearing it often. Then one day, when I was fifteen or sixteen years old, I suddenly realized, "Wait, you mean *me?* This is something *I* need to do?" It shed a whole new light on everything. I realized that confession of sin was not just the subject of a talk I had to listen to and agree with in a "Yeah, uh-huh" sort of way. I actually had to work on *applying* it throughout my own life.

Learning how to truly say "I'm sorry" is one of the most important lessons you will ever learn, and that is because it is basically a matter of learning how to be a genuinely honest and humble person. The two traits of honesty and humility always go together. Lewis makes it clear in the Narnia stories that the heroes are fundamentally honest, while the bad guys are fundamentally dishonest and proud. It is a basic characteristic of the divide between good and evil in Narnia just as it is in our world, so it is not surprising that the Narnia stories are full of illustrations of it.

# True Confessions

Although in this chapter I will go through the books in chronological order to highlight the theme, there are two common threads you can find in all these examples. The first is that confession of sin is all about honesty. The second is that people are constantly tempted to confess *others'* sins instead of their own, and that unlearning this natural instinct is a first step toward learning how to confess rightly.

## The Magician's Nephew

In *The Magician's Nephew,* remember that Digory and Polly are transported to the Wood Between the Worlds, and by jumping into various pools there they find they can travel to any one of hundreds of different worlds. The first one they visit is a dying world where they find a giant ruined city called Charn. In the central palace of this ruin is a great hall filled with great lords and ladies who are suspended (like "waxworks" Lewis says) in an enchanted sleep. And in the midst of the hall is a little golden hammer and a golden bell with this inscription:

> *Make your choice, adventurous Stranger;*
> *Strike the bell and bide the danger,*
> *Or wonder, till it drives you mad,*
> *What would have followed if you had.* (54)

Digory is by nature an intensely curious person—he will later grow up to be the wise old professor in *The Lion, the Witch and the Wardrobe*—and this inscription is just too much for him. He is immediately tempted to ring the bell. Polly, however, is not tempted at all. She not only does not care to find out what will happen if the bell is rung, but she also has a bad feeling about the whole thing. In the end they have a fight and Digory forcibly holds Polly out of the way while he rings the bell, which wakes the evil witch-queen Jadis (who later goes on to bring evil into Narnia).

When Polly later asks him to say he's sorry, Digory gives a kind of half-hearted confession:

> "Oh," said Digory, very surprised. "Well, all right, I'll say I'm sorry. And I really am sorry about what happened in the waxworks room. There: I've said I'm sorry. And now, do be decent and come back. I shall be in a frightful hole if you don't." (81)

First, he is giving the confession grudgingly, only after Polly demands it. Second, he says that he is sorry about "what happened," not about what he *did*. Third, he seems to be doing it mainly to stay on Polly's good side, so she will come back later and help him get Jadis back into her own world.

So Digory's foolish sin is not really dealt with until much later in the book when he, Polly, Jadis, and others find themselves in Narnia on the very day of its creation. Digory, seeing the magic of the new world, hopes that he will find a cure there for his dying mother, and he goes to Aslan for help. In order to do this, he has to tell the story of how he got into Narnia, but when he gets to the part about Jadis, he is less than honest:

> "[A]nd then we met the Witch in a place called Charn and she just held on to us when—"
>
> "You *met* the witch?" said Aslan in a low voice which had the threat of a growl in it. (147)

Notice that Digory is not telling an overt lie—he did meet the witch—but he is still leaving out some important parts of the story because it would reflect badly on his character to include those details.

> "She woke up," said Digory wretchedly. And then, turning very white, "I mean, I woke her. Because I wanted to know what would happen if I struck a bell. Polly didn't want to. It wasn't her fault. I—I fought her. I know I shouldn't have. I think I was a bit enchanted by the writing under the bell."
>
> "Do you?" asked Aslan; still speaking very low and deep.
>
> "No," said Digory, "I see now I wasn't. I was only pretending." (147)

Digory's guilt had even led him to lie to himself, such that he almost believed that he really was enchanted by the inscription on the bell. But in Aslan's presence, Digory cannot spin the story in his favor, gloss over his foolish sin, or tell any more lies. So he progresses quickly from spin to an honest confession. Aslan does not demand perfection from his servants, but he does demand honesty about their imperfections.

Following an honest confession, the next step for the offender (and the offended) is to make things right with honest forgiveness. So Aslan next turns to Polly:

> "And you, little Daughter. . . . Have you forgiven the Boy for the violence he did you in the Hall of Images in the desolate palace of accursed Charn?"
>
> "Yes, Aslan, we've made it up," said Polly. (152)

Part of confession is seeking forgiveness from those affected by your sin. Here, Aslan ensures that forgiveness has been honestly sought and freely given.

The moment of Digory's confession is as central to the story as the corresponding sin. Just as the sin brings the evil Jadis into the innocent world of Narnia, so the confession sets Digory on the path to being Aslan's servant, and equips him for the task that Aslan assigns to him in order to protect Narnia from that evil. Through Aslan, Lewis shows his readers how a full, honest confession—although it does not erase the earthly *consequences* of sin—does bring complete *forgiveness* and heals fractured relationships.

## THE LION, THE WITCH AND THE WARDROBE

At the beginning of *The Lion, the Witch and the Wardrobe,* Lucy is the first of her siblings to enter Narnia, and she is alone when it happens. Now when she gets back into our world, she tells Peter, Susan, and Edmund about it but of course they don't believe her—they think it is some kind of childish game (when they inspect the wardrobe after Lucy's return, it does not appear to be magical at all). Then not long afterward Edmund, who has been cruelly teasing Lucy about the whole thing, finds his way into Narnia as well and meets Lucy there. But when they return, Edmund is too proud to admit he was wrong, and too concerned with what the others think of him to risk getting ridiculed for believing Narnia is real. So he lies to Peter and Susan about it, saying he just played along with Lucy's game to humor her.

Lucy is heartbroken, and the others are now even more concerned that she is out of her mind. But when all four of them tumble through the wardrobe and Peter realizes that Lucy has been telling the truth the entire time, it is very interesting how he responds. He does not act sullen or proud; he does not begrudgingly admit that she was right. Instead, he immediately offers a complete apology:

> Peter turned at once to Lucy. "I apologize for not believing you. I'm sorry. Will you shake hands?"
> "Of course," said Lucy, and did. (55)

Now compare this to how Edmund had apologized in the same circumstance, just a bit earlier in the story when he himself had stumbled into Narnia for the first time. (Here, he thinks Lucy is somewhere nearby, when in fact she is too far away to even hear him.)

> "I say, Lu! I'm sorry I didn't believe you. I see now you were right all along. Do come out. Make it Pax."
> Still there was no answer.
> "Just like a girl," said Edmund to himself, "sulking somewhere, and won't accept an apology." (30)

He says the right words at first, but his apology is only on the surface, as we can see by his behavior right after this when he meets the witch. When he does meet Lucy later in Narnia, he offers a similarly insincere and proud half-apology: "I'll say I'm sorry if you like" (41). And after all four children make it into Narnia and Edmund's lie is found out, he is completely unrepentant:

> "Well, of all the poisonous little beasts—" said Peter, and shrugged his shoulders and said no more. There seemed, indeed, no more to say, and presently the four resumed their journey; but Edmund was saying to himself, "I'll pay you all out for this, you pack of stuck-up, self-satisfied prigs." (56)

This attitude eats away at Edmund for the entire first half of the book. He just gets crankier and more sullen with his siblings until the moment when he sneaks away to betray them to the witch.

This betrayal, and Edmund's eventual redemption by Aslan's sacrifice, is the core symbol of the book, representing all of humanity's sinfulness. And it all starts with the kind of heart that hates quick, honest confession.

## The Horse and His Boy

In *The Horse and His Boy,* Shasta is a prince of Archenland who is lost as a child and raised as a poor fisherman's son in Calormen. When he is about to be sold as a slave by his adoptive father, he runs away with a talking Narnian horse named Bree. They meet up with a young Calormene lady named Aravis and her horse Hwin (also a Narnian horse), and decide that they will escape together to Narnia. Along the way they discover a Calormene plot to invade Archenland, which sits between Calormen and Narnia, and they find themselves racing against the invading troops to warn Archenland of the impending slaughter.

Just as they are almost exhausted, Aslan appears suddenly and chases them in order to give them the last push of energy they need to complete their journey. They believe he is an ordinary wild lion, so they run for their lives. Aslan soon catches up with Hwin and Aravis and gives Aravis a swipe across the back with his claws. (This is poetic justice; Aravis had previously caused one of her own servant girls to receive ten lashes that she did not deserve.)

Seeing this, Shasta, who grew up in a poor fisherman's hut and knows nothing about fighting or nobility or courage, urges Bree to turn back to help Aravis and Hwin. When Bree apparently does not hear him, he jumps off Bree's back and runs back to confront the lion with nothing but his bare hands. At this, the lion surprises everyone by running away, allowing them to find refuge with an old hermit in the forest.

Shasta's action evokes two interesting and very different responses from Aravis and Bree. Bree is humiliated, since he thought of himself as a brave warhorse, and yet fled from the lion that Shasta confronted. Aravis, meanwhile, has acted rudely to Shasta for most of their time together; she has made it clear that she considers herself far above him in every respect. But after this event, her attitude has changed:

> "We all ran as hard as we could," said Hwin.
> "Shasta didn't!" snorted Bree. "At least he ran in the right direction: ran *back.* . . ."
> "I know," said Aravis, "I felt just the same. Shasta was marvelous. I'm just as bad as you, Bree. I've been snubbing him and looking down on him ever since you met us and now he turns out to be the best of us all. But I think it would be better to stay and say we're sorry than to go back to Calormen." (150–151)

In other words, Aravis is not too proud to admit she is wrong about Shasta, and she wisely sees that apologizing to Shasta and being taken down a notch while living freely in Narnia and Archenland is far better than keeping her pride while returning to the slavish culture of Calormen.

Bree's response is quite different, and again confession is at the heart of it. The lion incident has humiliated Bree, who despite being a trained warhorse had kept running in order to save his own skin. Throughout the book, Bree has shown himself to be very conceited—he is, after all, an intelligent Narnian horse who has lived too long among the ordinary dumb horses of Calormen. Living like this for almost his whole life, and being a very valuable horse owned by a great Calormene lord, has puffed him up. This is why he is so utterly ashamed by Shasta's act of courage in contrast to his own act of cowardice. In fact, he spends a good deal of time feeling sorry for himself—which is not at all the same thing as being sorry for his sins. Eventually the wise old hermit whom they are staying with offers this advice:

> "My good Horse, you've lost nothing but your self-conceit. No, no, cousin. Don't put back your ears and shake your mane at me. If you are really so humbled as you sounded a minute ago, you must learn to listen to sense." (151)

This is an important lesson that modern people need to learn. There is a type of person who makes a mistake and decides he is going to mope around afterwards with a little black rain cloud over his head. It's just like the old children's song: "Nobody likes me, everybody hates me, I guess I'll go eat worms." Does he do this because he really is going to go eat worms? Does he honestly thinks he is a total, worthless failure? No, he does it because his pride has been hurt and he wants people to pay attention to him. He wants others to gather around him and tell him he is not only *not* a failure, he is in fact a very wonderful and special person. Instead of humbling himself and offering a genuine apology, this type of person hides behind extreme false humility ("I'm worthless") in order to get an ego boost from those around him.

So is Bree sad because he is genuinely sorry for his sins? No. He is sad because his pride has suffered a blow. He seems sorry, but it is not the same as true confession. Fortunately, the hermit will not indulge him, and neither does Aslan, who puts Bree completely right a bit later on.

> "Now, Bree," [Aslan] said, "you poor, proud, frightened Horse, draw near. . . ."

"Aslan," said Bree in a shaken voice, "I'm afraid I must be rather a fool."

"Happy the Horse who knows that while he is still young." (201)

## PRINCE CASPIAN

In *Prince Caspian*, Peter, Susan, Edmund, and Lucy are called back to Narnia centuries after they ruled as kings and queens there (at the end of *The Lion, the Witch and the Wardrobe*). They arrive in the ruins of Cair Paravel, where they meet Trumpkin the dwarf and learn about Caspian. From there they must travel back to the place where Caspian is besieged by Miraz, but the journey is by no means an easy one. Midway through, Aslan appears only to Lucy, who is always the most spiritually sensitive of the four, and shows her the path they should follow. But to the others who do not see Aslan, that path looks much more difficult than their other option. So even though Edmund sides with Lucy, Peter and Susan overrule them and decide to take the easier path. Lucy is very upset not only because they do not believe her but also because she must disobey Aslan in order to stay with the others. Eventually, however, the seemingly easy path is filled with unseen difficulties and they end up needing to backtrack to where they started, losing critical time in the process.

At last Aslan appears to all of them, showing that Lucy was right all along. Susan's apology is a wonderful example of pure, honest confession:

"I'm sorry. . . . But I've been far worse than you know. I really believed it was him . . . deep down inside." (152)

She doesn't just say she is sorry for not believing Lucy; she confesses the additional sin of doing so in spite of her own deep conviction that Lucy was right. It is pretty clear from the story that Susan did not *want* to believe Lucy because she was upset that Aslan would show himself to Lucy only at first. It is this additional sin of pride and self-deception that she is confessing here. Even though she could have just stopped at "I'm sorry," she recognizes that there were deeper heart issues involved. This is real honesty.

Peter's apology is also straightforward. As soon as he sees Aslan he says, "I've been leading them wrong." He does not try to make excuses (such as, "But *we* couldn't see you, and the other path *looked* easier—why didn't you just show yourself to all of us then?"). Neither does he try to blame anyone besides himself. This is good, because Aslan tends to growl at those who try to shift blame, while he immediately and fully forgives those who accept responsibility with an honest confession.

## The Voyage of the Dawn Treader

Near the ending of *The Voyage of the Dawn Treader,* the ship reaches the "utter East"—the very end of the world—and Caspian is so enthralled with the prospect of going into Aslan's Country for more adventures that he says he will abdicate his throne and never return to Narnia. But his friends will not allow him to do that. Why not? Remember when we discussed authority in *The Horse and His Boy:* King Lune would not allow Shasta (now Prince Corin) to avoid the future kingship. The law is above the king, and just as a sentry would be disobedient to leave his post, so a king would be disobedient to leave his office. So even though Caspian has authority over everyone on the ship, his friends know that the law is above the king, and they tell him that he is not allowed to go on.

> "You are the King of Narnia [said Reepicheep]. . . . You
> shall not please yourself with adventures as if you were
> a private person." (239)

Caspian knows they are right, but he loses his temper anyway, insults his old friend Reepicheep, and stomps away to his cabin.

Soon he returns to the others, telling them that Aslan appeared to him in his cabin and set him right. He is very sobered by it, but he does not delay in apologizing fully:

> "It's no good," he said. "I might as well have behaved
> decently for all the good I did with my temper and
> swagger." (240)

Caspian does not try to gloss over his behavior at all; he calls it exactly what it was: "temper and swagger."

## THE SILVER CHAIR

Remember that Eustace first appeared in *The Voyage of the Dawn Treader,* where he starts out as a first-rate stinker but is eventually converted by Aslan into a good character. He and his friend Jill then become the main characters in *The Silver Chair,* which is chronologically the next book in the Narnia series.

At the start of the book, Eustace and Jill are pulled by magic out of their awful school (aptly named "Experiment House") to Aslan's Country in the utter East of Narnia. After a bit of exploring they find themselves at the edge of a huge precipice. Eustace, who has a fear of heights, immediately turns white and jerks her back from the edge. But Jill, despising Eustace for his fear, tries to one-up him by standing too close to the edge. But when she actually looks down from the cliff, it is like no cliff that could ever exist in our world—it is miles above the clouds and seems to just keep going down forever. When her head starts to spin and she almost loses her balance, Eustace overcomes his own fear to bring her back from the edge. There is a brief, confused struggle and Eustace goes over the edge, screaming. At this point Aslan suddenly appears and blows Eustace away toward Narnia.

Jill is in shock, but her first real reaction is interesting—she tries to convince herself that it wasn't her fault. But when she speaks with Aslan just a few pages later, does her explanation work out?

> "Human Child," said the Lion, "Where is the Boy?"
> "He fell over the cliff," said Jill, and added, "Sir." She didn't know what else to call him, and it sounded cheek to call him nothing.
> "How did he come to do that, Human Child?" (24)

Aslan is not asking for information; he saw Eustace fall. But this is the type of thing Aslan is interested in. He wants people to tell the parts of the story that they would conveniently leave out if they were telling it to anyone else. He is interested in whether people will confess and tell the whole truth, or spin it to cover up anything that might reflect badly on them. So how does Jill measure up?

> "He was trying to stop me from falling, Sir."
> "Why were you so near the edge, Human Child?"
> "I was showing off, Sir."
> "That is a very good answer, Human Child. Do so no more." (24)

Aslan does not allow Jill to gloss over this part of the story. He questions her in such a way that she must either confess the truth honestly or tell an outright lie. To Jill's credit, she chooses to confess honestly and without excuses.

And once she confesses, Aslan does not harp on the sin or its bad consequences. He does not rub it in with a statement like, "You know Eustace would have died because of your foolishness if I had not been there." He simply says, "Do so no more." Of course, there are still consequences to Jill's sin—she now has to learn the signs for seeking Prince Rilian all by herself, and they arrive too late in Narnia to get help from the dying Caspian. Aslan requires Jill to deal with the consequences, but he does not keep dwelling on the sin itself and neither would he want Jill to.

As the book progresses, Eustace and Jill squabble frequently with each other. Near the end of the book, they have finally found the end of their quest but they are trapped deep underground and it does not look like they will be able to get out. Eustace takes the opportunity to make sure there is no unconfessed sin between them:

> But when Scrubb shook hands with Jill, he said, "So long Jill. Sorry I've been a funk and so ratty. I hope you get safe home," and Jill said, "So long, Eustace. And I'm sorry I've been such a pig." And this was the first time they had ever used Christian names, because one didn't do it at school. (191)

Although I would never recommend saving up confession until a life-threatening situation arises, it is still quite right for Eustace and Jill to "make up" on such an occasion. Confession is better late than never.

Finally, at the end of the book when their quest is finished, Eustace and Jill find themselves back in Aslan's country where they meet him again:

> And in less time than it takes to breathe Jill forgot about the dead king of Narnia and remembered only how she had made Eustace fall over the cliff, and how she had

helped to muff nearly all the signs, and about all the snappings and quarrellings. And she wanted to say "I'm sorry" but she could not speak. Then the Lion drew them toward him with his eyes, and bent down and touched their pale faces with his tongue, and said:

"Think of that no more. I will not always be scolding. You have done the work for which I sent you into Narnia." (236)

Being in Aslan's presence naturally creates a posture of confession in Jill. She does not feel sorry for her faults because she has a list of sins and is methodically checking them off—she feels sorry because she *knows* Aslan, and seeing him makes her realize how being a quarreling sort of person is deeply inconsistent with Aslan's character. He is not an impersonal force behind a list of dead laws. He is a person, and sin can be easily identified by asking yourself, "Is he that way, or is he not?"

As soon as she realizes this she wants to confess all the things she has done wrong, but it is wonderful that Aslan interrupts her. He knows her heart, and he gives comfort and praise instead of scolding. That is the pattern of how Aslan receives all those who offer him honest confession. Aslan cares about confession of sin, but there is always something beyond it. In other words, being honest about our faults and failings is like washing up for dinner, so you can enjoy that dinner with clean hands. But imagine if someone just washed up for dinner, all the time, over and over, and never came to the table? Washing is important, but the point of being clean is so that we can enjoy the meal.

## THE LAST BATTLE

Near the end of *The Last Battle,* Shift has succeeded in convincing some of the Narnians to worship a false god he has made by combining Aslan with the Calormene god Tash—"Tashlan." Eventually, their behavior actually summons Tash, who is an evil creature with four arms and a vulture's head. Up to this point, Puzzle the donkey has gone along with Shift's schemes (dressing up in a lion skin and pretending to be Aslan), not because he is malicious but because he is naïve, weak, and easily manipulated. But when Puzzle finally sees Tash and realizes the evil he has helped bring on Narnia, he says, "I see now that I really have been a very bad donkey" (95). To his credit, Puzzle does not try to wriggle out of taking responsibility for what he has done. He does not try to excuse himself and put all the blame on Shift. He admits, rightly, that he should have known better and stood up to Shift.

Another example of confession in *The Last Battle* is similar to Eustace and Jill's "farewell confession" that we saw earlier. Here, the Narnian king Tirian and his faithful unicorn Jewel make sure their accounts are settled before they go to battle:

> "Kiss me, Jewel," he said. "For certainly this is our last night on earth. And if ever I offended against you in any matter great or small, forgive me now."
> "Dear king," said the unicorn, "I could almost wish you had, so that I might forgive it." (111)

Again, this type of confession in dire circumstances is not going to be the norm for our lives, but it shows again that Aslan's servants value short accounts. They never want to say goodbye to someone if there is an unresolved sin between them.

# False Confessions

Thus far in this chapter we have seen examples of good, honest confessions. Now let's look at the other side of the coin and see how Lewis handles false confessions.

Early on in *The Voyage of the Dawn Treader*, Eustace is still an unconverted first-rate stinker, and he gets the nasty idea of grabbing Reepicheep, the two-foot tall talking mouse, by the tail and swinging him around. But he gravely underestimates Reepicheep, who manages to draw his sword, stab Eustace's hand, pick himself up off the deck, and challenge Eustace to a duel over the dishonor and insult he had given. Now Eustace is a faux-pacifist coward, and when he realizes that everyone seems to take the idea of a duel quite seriously, he realizes that the only way out is to apologize to Reepicheep, which he does "sulkily" (35). He is not sorry at all, and in fact he blames everyone but himself for the incident, so his confession is completely phony. This tendency to blame everyone else continues to be one of Eustace's central faults until his conversion: "And there they sat in the straw and wondered what was happening to Caspian and tried to stop Eustace talking as if everyone except himself was to blame" (45).

In *The Magician's Nephew*, recall how Aslan led Digory to confess his sin of fighting with Polly and waking the evil witch. But long before that honest confession, Digory had already failed to give a proper apology for his actions. Just after he and Polly return home from the Wood Between the Worlds and accidentally let the witch loose in London, Digory asks Polly to help him fix the mess.

> "I shall go home by the tunnel," said Polly rather coldly. . . . "And if you want me to come back, hadn't you better say you're sorry?"

"Sorry?" exclaimed Digory. "Well now, if that isn't just like a girl! What have I done?"

"Oh nothing of course," said Polly sarcastically. "Only nearly screwed my wrist off in that room with all the waxworks, like a cowardly bully. Only struck the bell with the hammer, like a silly idiot. Only turned back in the wood so that she had time to catch hold of you . . . That's all."

"Oh," said Digory, very surprised. "Well, all right, I'll say I'm sorry." (80–81)

Digory's first reaction is to deny he has done anything wrong—he has completely blinded himself to the facts. Only when Polly lays out the facts again does he grudgingly admit she may have a point.

Later in the same book we see the final destination of those who refuse to repent throughout their whole lives. When Uncle Andrew enters Narnia, he hates everything about it because he is wicked and the newly-made world is perfectly good—unbearably good to people like him. Lewis writes, "If he could have got away from it by creeping into a rat's hole, he would have done so" (108). But since there is no rat hole, Uncle Andrew must do the next-best thing: put his hands over his ears and lie to himself. Later on, he keeps repeating to himself "Animals can't talk" over and over again, until he finally makes himself believe it. From that point on, whenever an animal talks, Uncle Andrew only hears roaring or barking or chirping. He has cut himself off from reality. As Aslan says, "Oh, Adam's sons, how cleverly you defend yourselves against all that might do you good!" (185). What Uncle Andrew needs is pure, straightforward honesty. He needs to confess his evil deeds and recognize the goodness of Aslan. In refusing, he shows that he would rather live in self-deception than do that. His punishment is nothing more than having Aslan grant his wish.

We already talked a bit about Peter's honest apology to Lucy at the beginning of *The Lion, the Witch and the Wardrobe* when he discovers that Lucy was telling the truth about Narnia being a real place. Here I want to focus more on Edmund's false apology. When Edmund first stumbles into Narnia, he thinks Lucy is in earshot, so he calls out for her. When she does not answer:

> "Just like a girl," said Edmund to himself, "sulking somewhere, and won't accept an apology." (30)

He is standing in the middle of the woods, and Lucy is nowhere in sight. For all he knows, she may be lost or eaten by a bear. But he immediately jumps to the conclusion that she is sulking. This shows two things: first, that his own apology is inadequate, having some of the right words but no depth of sincerity; and second, that he is trying to blame her for wrongdoing so as to shift the focus away from his own faults as quickly as possible.

When he finally does meet up with Lucy, is his attitude any better?

> "All right," said Edmund, "I see you were right and it is a magic wardrobe after all. I'll say I'm sorry if you like. But where on earth have you been all this time? I've been looking for you everywhere." (41)

That little "if you like" speaks volumes. It means he is not acknowledging any real wrongdoing, and is implying that he'll only apologize if she explicitly says she wants him to—and (he implies) that would probably be a very unreasonable and self-centered thing for her to do. He is trying to force her into *demanding* an apology, casting her (in his own mind) as some kind of difficult person who is too easily offended and needs to be humored. Again, he is not being honest or taking responsibility; he is trying to shift the focus away from himself by implying that she is really the one with the problem. And notice that he does not even wait for her reply—he immediately demands to know where she's been (again, as if it is her fault they have been separated all this time).

Because Edmund refuses to apologize honestly, he cruelly betrays Lucy by pretending to the others that he and Lucy had only been pretending.

> "Oh, Edmund, I *am* glad you've got in too. The others will have to believe in Narnia now that both of us have been there. What fun it will be!"
>
> But Edmund secretly thought that it would not be as good fun for him as for her. He would have to admit that Lucy had been right, before all the others, and he felt sure that the others would all be on the side of the Fauns and the animals; but he was already more than half on the side of the Witch. (43)

Edmund knows that if he tells the truth, he will have to say he was wrong in front of Peter and the others. He also suspects that his allegiance to the White Witch will come out sooner or later, and he wants to keep that covered up as long as possible.

So Edmund's feeble, phony apologies do nothing but whitewash his rotten deceptions and pride. The lesson here is that apologies are only effective when they are completely honest and humbling.

Another important lesson that Narnia teaches about confession is this: Confess your own sin, not your neighbor's. We have already talked about Peter's honest confession in *Prince Caspian* when he admits he did not believe that Lucy really saw Aslan. But in the same passage, Lucy herself (who was in the right all along) slips up and starts blaming the others:

"Yes, wasn't it a shame?" said Lucy. "*I* saw you all right. They wouldn't believe me. They're all so—"

From somewhere deep in Aslan's body came the faintest suggestion of a growl. (142)

Instead of just letting the others confess their own sins to Aslan, Lucy here is hauling them out and holding them up in front of her, essentially saying, "*I* was obedient all along, but *they* weren't!" Aslan does not tolerate that kind of talk; he does not want his servants confessing other people's sins.

He does not stop there—he needs to show Lucy that she wasn't so obedient after all:

"But it wasn't my fault anyway, was it?"

The Lion looked straight into her eyes.

"Oh, Aslan," said Lucy. "You don't mean it was? How could I—I couldn't have left the others and come up to you alone, how could I? Don't look at me like that . . . oh well, I suppose I *could*." (142)

Not only did Lucy try to confess the sins of others, she tried to do so when she had unconfessed sin herself. She should have obeyed and followed Aslan, even though the others did not believe her. She tries to convince herself that nothing bad that happened was her fault, but in fact she does share the blame.

## Conclusion

It is remarkable how often the subject of confession turns up in Narnia. The central themes that tie it all together are these: first, that good confession is honest and humbling, and that means you are not to spin, cover, gloss over, or make excuses; second, that God fully and immediately forgives those who do confess honestly; and third, that every person is responsible for confessing his own sins—not his neighbors'.

What is also remarkable is how Lewis can take a subject like "confession of sin" and make the right lessons come out naturally as he tells the stories. When you learn about confession in Narnia, you are not sitting in church listening to a sermon, or attending a conference, or taking a practical Christianity course at school. Of course those are all good things to do, but the method of teaching and the way you apply it is different when you learn through a story.

When you learn something from a story, you don't think something like, "Well, I have to make sure I follow the five-step process for making a good confession of sin . . . now what was that fourth step again?" Instead, you learn somewhere deep down that you don't want to be an Edmund; you want to be a Peter. You don't want to point fingers like Lucy did when the others wouldn't believe she saw Aslan. You know that using excuses shows poor character because that's how Eustace acted. You want to tell the whole story, and not gloss over your own failings, because that's how Digory and Polly acted with Aslan. The more you read stories like this, the more these lessons settle deep down in your bones, and the more you see yourself as a character in your own story. It is a very good exercise to occasionally stop and think, "If my life were a story, am I being an admirable character right now or not?" It is amazing how many layers of petty self-justification this thought alone can wash away.

That is why I would encourage you to read and reread these stories over and over again, and model your behavior on the characters you admire. When you need guidance about what to do when there is some squabble at school, or if your parents ask you about an incident you were involved in and you are tempted to gloss over whatever might reflect badly on yourself, you will know almost instinctively what to do. And when you are tempted to do the wrong thing anyway, you should think of Aslan and the "faintest suggestion of a growl."

At the beginning of this chapter I said that confession of sin might seem like a dreary subject. By now you should see that it is not that way at all. Honest confession makes it possible for imperfect people to live in fellowship with one another as friends, siblings, parents, children, and neighbors. Without confession, a backlog of sin just keeps building up until it destroys relationships and destroys lives. Confession and forgiveness, far from being dreary subjects to learn, are the most fundamental and liberating lessons in the Christian life, and I am deeply grateful that the Narnia stories are able to teach them in such a clear, effective, and vibrant way.

CHAPTER 3

# NOBILITY

NOBILITY IS A word whose meaning has been largely lost in our culture. What does it mean to be noble? Just as with concepts like authority and confession, there are two sides to the coin—a true nobility and a false nobility. There are also characters with no nobility whatsoever. King Peter is an example of true nobility. Jadis of Charn has a certain grandeur that we might mistake for nobility, but at its heart it is rotten and empty. And Eustace, when we first meet him, is the quintessential modern child who has no concept of nobility at all.

The concept of nobility is foreign to many modern Americans. We are like Shasta in *The Horse and His Boy,* who "had . . . no idea of how noble and freeborn people behave" (75). Now Shasta, as you recall, is a prince of Archenland who is brought up from infancy as a Calormene peasant, the adopted son of a fisherman. After he runs away with Bree and Hwin and Aravis, he visits Calormen's capital Tashbaan for the first time and is amazed by its size and wealth. He also catches his first glimpse of Narnians (whom he thought of as foreigners), and this sight impresses him in a very different way.

Most of them had legs bare to the knee. Their tunics were of fine, bright, hardy colors—woodland green, or gay yellow, or fresh blue. . . . A few were bare-headed. The swords at their sides were long and straight, not curved like Calormene scimitars. And instead of being grave and mysterious like most Calormenes, they walked with a swing and let their arms and shoulders go free, and chatted and laughed. One was whistling. You could see that they were ready to be friends with anyone who was friendly and didn't give a fig for anyone who wasn't. Shasta thought he'd never seen anything so lovely in his life. (57–58)

Lewis is making a very pointed contrast here between the Narnian and Calormene societies, and he is trying to create a picture of true nobility. The Calormene civilization is full of great power, wealth, and impressive achievements, but it is all under the oppressive authority of the Tisroc and the god Tash. As we saw in the previous chapter on authority, it is a society of slaves. The Narnians certainly have and wield authority as well, but it is the authority of law over a free people, not the authority of a supreme leader over his servants. The Narnians walk down the streets—even the kings and queens—but the great lords and ladies of Calormen are carried around in litters by their slaves, forcing common people aside whenever they pass. The Calormenes cultivate a kind of grave aloofness; earlier Shasta had noted the city's collection of "great statues of the gods and heroes of Calormen—who are mostly impressive rather than agreeable to look at" (56). Calormen is impressive but oppressive. The Narnians, in contrast, are bold while remaining friendly and open. Calormene nobility says, "I'm better than you, so get out of my way." Narnian nobility says, "Let's have a walk together, because I'm free and you're free."

# Nobility is Merry

Another thing that is clear from this description is that Narnian nobility is merry. It is a shame that most of us only use the word *merry* to say "Merry Christmas" once a year. Being merry is such an important Christian virtue that we really ought to use the word more often. In *The Voyage of the Dawn Treader,* the ship lands on the Lone Islands where they meet with Lord Bern, one of the lost friends of Caspian's father. Lewis describes Bern's household thus: "Bern and his gracious wife and merry daughters made them good cheer" (49–50). A short time later, Caspian rids the islands of the grumpy, greedy, negligent, despotic bureaucrat that had previously ruled them, and he installs Bern as duke in his place. You can tell Lewis doesn't think much of governors and bureaucrats; they have no nobility. What the Lone Islands need, according to Lewis, is not a stuffy bureaucrat but a noble duke with a merry family that likes to laugh around the dinner table.

At the end of *The Horse and His Boy,* notice how Lewis describes King Lune's royal feast to celebrate the defeat of Rabadash:

> And the wine flowed and tales were told and jokes were cracked, and then silence was made and the King's poet with two fiddlers stepped out into the middle of the circle. Aravis and Cor prepared themselves to be bored, for the poetry they knew was the Calormene kind, and you know now what that was like. (221)

He is referring to a passage earlier in the book where Narnian and Archenlander poetry is described as thrilling—all about "love and war"—while Calormene poetry was dull and dusty—all "choice apophthegms and useful maxims" (117). So Aravis and Cor are surprised when the poetry is actually not only comprehensible but also full of joy and excitement. This is another instance of Lewis showing us that nobility is not about being grave and fussy all the time—it is about jokes, poems, dancing, music, and feasting.

I want to take a quick side trail at this point regarding Lewis's contrast of Narnia and Calormen. It is tempting for some modern readers to object that Lewis is always putting Calormen in a bad light because he has an axe to grind with oriental cultures and wants to show how superior western cultures are in comparison. While there is some truth in that objection (Lewis *does* think the Christian west is superior and is not shy about it), it is only fair to note that he makes a few contrasts that go in the opposite direction. For example, in this passage he points out the weak culture of storytelling in the west compared to oriental cultures (which Calormen represents):

> For in Calormen, story-telling (whether the stories are true or made up) is a thing you're taught, just as English boys and girls are taught essay writing. The difference is that people want to hear the stories, whereas I never heard of anyone who wanted to read the essays. (35)

## Nobility and Appearance

Nobility even affects the way that characters look. In *The Silver Chair,* when the two children and Puddleglum and Prince Rilian tunnel out of the ground and right into a Narnian snow dance, the Narnians immediately recognize Rilian as noble.

> For now they saw the Prince. . . . That look is in the face of all true Kings of Narnia, who rule by the will of

Aslan and sit at Cair Paravel on the throne of Peter the
High King. (224–225)

Nobility in the heart and mind is reflected in Rilian's
external appearance; the state of one's heart and mind
work their way out to the physical level.

It goes the other way too—ignoble characters start to
look more and more unpleasant. In *The Lion, the Witch
and the Wardrobe,* when Edmund first enters Narnia, the
first person he meets is the White Witch, who wants to use
him to find his siblings so that she can kill them and avert
the prophecy of her downfall. So she flatters him, feeds
him enchanted Turkish Delight, and manipulates his selfish, rotten attitude toward his brother and sisters until he
agrees to bring them all into her house. Much later, when
he has slipped away from the beavers' house to betray his
brother and sisters to the witch, Mr. Beaver says:

> "I didn't like to mention it before (he being your brother
> and all) but the moment I set eyes on that brother of yours
> I said to myself 'Treacherous.' He had the look of one
> who has been with the Witch and eaten her food." (85)

Disloyalty is one of the most basic ways to reject nobility,
and Edmund's treachery is quickly written on his face.

One of the functions of a good story is to make certain
things explicit, external, and obvious that are more difficult to see in real life. Lewis knows how to do this, which
is why nobility and treachery can be seen at a glance in
Narnia. Of course, the same is often true in our world as
well, but the people who discern it have to be careful to
keep it to themselves. They might find themselves being
sued for the discriminatory practice of "lookism."

## Nobility and Loyalty

Noble people always keep their word. In *Prince Caspian,* remember that Nikabrik the dwarf starts out on Caspian's side, but later we see that he is really just looking out for himself and his own dwarf clan. When this starts becoming clear, someone reminds him that he took an oath of loyalty to Caspian. In response to this, he sneers, "Court manners, court manners" (165). In other words, he makes light of his oaths and loyalties as nothing more than empty words, and he mocks those who think that such formalities mean anything. This is not true of a noble character who would always keep his word and loyalties.

## Nobility and Sacrifice

We have already seen from chapter one that real authority requires self-sacrifice, but the same is true of real nobility. And as with authority, Aslan provides the clearest example and ultimate definition of nobility. In *The Lion, the Witch and the Wardrobe,* Aslan—the most noble figure in the story—gives himself in exchange for Edmund, who is at this point the most ignoble character in the story.

Modern people have forgotten this. We moderns tend to think of "nobility" as involving self-centered aristocrats parading around with their noses in the air. Even most Christians have lost sight of what the word means, despite the apostle Paul telling us in Philippians that "whatever is lovely, whatever is *noble,* whatever is of good report— meditate on those things" (4:8). In this passage, we are directly commanded to strive for nobility and to admire that which is noble.

But the devil tries to confuse us by slandering nobility; he wants us to think that nobility describes the sort of stuck- up, proud person who won't associate with lesser beings.

And that becomes an easy excuse to cover up unrighteousness—"I don't want to be like that goody-two-shoes who thinks he's better than everyone else." Of course, such stuck-up nobility is counterfeit nobility. Think about that for a moment—what does *counterfeiting* mean, and why do people do it? Counterfeiting is making a fake copy of something valuable. Criminals make counterfeit money because they can buy real stuff with it. But nobody goes into their basement and counterfeits Safeway shopping bags, because they are not worth anything. Now it would be very silly for someone to think that hundred-dollar bills are worthless because counterfeits exist. On the contrary, the very existence of counterfeits proves that the originals *are* worth something. In the same way, the fact that false nobility exists should not cause us to reject true nobility; it should remind us how valuable true nobility really is. And, getting back to our main point: false nobility is puffed up, while true nobility is sacrificial.

Prince Rilian is a good example of this sacrifice. Near the end of *The Silver Chair,* he, Eustace, Jill, and Puddleglum are deep underground in the Underland and surrounded by hordes of earthmen, and they are not sure if they are going to make it out alive.

> "But won't the others all come rushing at us . . . ?" said Jill in a voice not so steady as she tried to make it.
> "Then, Madam," said the Prince, "You shall see us die fighting around you, and you must commend yourself to the Lion." (197)

Rilian is in a very dangerous situation, but his first thought is not for himself. It is for protecting the lady nearest him with his life. The Narnians are always a chivalrous people, and the heart of real chivalry is self-sacrifice.

A similar situation comes up in *The Horse and His Boy.* Recall that Rabadash, the Calormene prince, had visited Cair Paravel and was attempting to court Queen Susan. In a diplomatic gesture, the Narnian kings and queens and their entourage make a follow-up visit to Tashbaan. Now while Rabadash had been extremely charming when in Narnia, his true colors are revealed on his home turf, and Queen Susan decides that she could never consider marrying him. But they all perceive that when Rabadash finds out, things are going to turn ugly and the outlook for the small group of Narnians, isolated in Calormen's capital city, does not look good. This is what King Peter has to say:

> "As to that," said the King, "I do not doubt that every one of us would sell our lives dearly in the gate and they would not come at the Queen but over our dead bodies." (70)

There is no hesitation; the first instinct of a noble person is to do one's duty even if it means sacrificing his own life for someone else's.

A third example comes from *The Last Battle.* Cair Paravel has fallen to the Calormenes, and Tirian, the last king of Narnia, gets a message from Roonwit the centaur, who has just died in battle. The messenger says:

> I was with him in his last hour and he gave me this message to your Majesty: to remember that all worlds draw to an end and that noble death is a treasure which no one is too poor to buy. (103)

You do not have to be a king, or a rich man, or any type of great leader in order to be noble in this way. Nobility is not about wealth; it is about what kind of character you are and what kind of actions you take.

# Nobility as Gift

We have seen so far how nobility involves duty, sacrifice, merriment, and freedom. People who are becoming noble are following the example of Aslan, but it is also very important to see that these people are not able to do this under their own power. The ability to follow Aslan faithfully is itself a gift from Aslan.

In *Prince Caspian*, when the Narnians are slowly losing the siege to Miraz's greater army, they decide that trying to end the battle by single combat—Peter versus Miraz—is their best chance. Of course, it is a long shot because Miraz would have to be crazy to give up his army's advantage and risk losing everything on the outcome of a single duel. But Edmund is sent to deliver the challenge, and in the end, Miraz's treacherous advisors goad him into it by insinuating that he will lose face if he refuses to fight a mere boy. For my point right now, the key part of this passage is how Aslan imparts a visible nobility to Edmund in order to give weight to his message: "Aslan had breathed on him at their meeting and a kind of greatness hung about him" (179). When Miraz's advisors see him, they say, "He is a kinglier man than ever Miraz was."

The Bible uses similar language in many places. God gave Solomon "majesty" (1 Chr. 29:25). This was to show the people that Solomon was not just a man sitting on a throne who somehow tricked everyone into thinking he had actual authority. Rather, God gave him the spirit to rule. Nobility is a gift from God, not something that we can just trump up within ourselves.

# Nobility and Humility

Our stereotypes of "nobility" tend to associate it with pride. But that is only true of false nobility; real nobility is always humble. The old expression *noblesse oblige*, meaning "nobility obliges," captures this nicely. Rank is more a matter of responsibility than privilege.

When (in *The Voyage of the Dawn Treader*) Eustace, Lucy, and Edmund tumble through a painting into Narnia, they are hauled up out of the ocean into Caspian's ship. Now it is a small ship without many private cabins, but Caspian is first in line to humble himself by giving his cabin to Lucy. Even when Lord Drinian, the ship's captain, begs Caspian not to take a lesser cabin, Caspian insists (25). A proud king would have told one of his underlings to be moved, muttering that "kings have certain privileges, after all," but Caspian is not like that—he volunteers to take the lower place, the place that in the world's eyes has less honor.

The ignoble character of Eustace stands in direct contrast to Caspian's. In one of the book's most humorous passages, Lewis gives us excerpts from Eustace's diary, where we see he has no respect for Caspian's noble office: "They call him a King. I said I was a Republican but he had to ask me what that meant! He doesn't seem to know anything at all" (31). And we see the same lack of nobility in Eustace's attitude toward women, as he describes how he objected to Caspian's preferential treatment of Lucy: "C. [Caspian] says that's because she's a girl. I tried to make him see what Alberta [Eustace's mother] says, that all that sort of thing is really lowering girls, but he was too dense" (31). Eustace would like to believe in the type of gender equality that means he personally has to sacrifice as little as possible. In his perfect world, he would "honor" women by *not* giving preferential treatment to them. He is trying to turn his own self-centeredness into the moral high ground of "fairness for everybody."

## The False Nobility of Jadis

I mentioned earlier in this chapter that Jadis is a character that one might think of as noble, and I want to explore this further. To start with, what kind of a place was her kingdom, Charn? When Digory and Polly arrive there, they find an old, dead world with a giant red sun. Her descriptions of its former glory give us a good picture of what it was like under her rule:

> "That is the door to the dungeons," she would say, or "That passage leads to the principal torture chambers," or "This was the old banqueting hall where my great-grandfather bade seven hundred nobles to a feast and killed them all before they had drunk their fill. They had had rebellious thoughts." . . .
>
> "It is silent now. But I have stood here when the whole air was full of the noises of Charn; the trampling of feet, the creaking of wheels, the cracking of the whips and the groaning of slaves, the thunder of chariots, and the sacrificial drums beating in the temples." (61, 65)

Clearly Charn was a very great city. It is not only enormous but filled with impressive architecture and wealth. Yet it has none of the true nobility of Narnia, because it is pure power without goodness. It is cruel. When Digory and Polly looked at all the images of the kings and queens of Charn, the earlier ones looked like kind, gracious people; the later ones were still noble-seeming but cruel; and at the end of the line was Jadis, cruelest of all.

You cannot despise or belittle Charn, but nevertheless Lewis paints it and its ruler as very evil. The culmination of both Jadis's power and evil was her use of the Deplorable Word—one word which, if used by a powerful magician, would destroy all life except the one who spoke it. Now all the great and powerful of Charn had agreed that no matter how much they fought amongst themselves, no one would ever use that particular weapon. And no one had, until Jadis fought a great civil war against her sister. Her sister stormed the city, then the palace, then the very room where Jadis waited. But just when it looked like she had triumphed, Jadis spoke the Deplorable Word. Rather than lose the kingdom, she preferred to annihilate all life on her planet.*

Although Lewis makes it very clear that Jadis is an evil person, he does not turn her into a caricature. She is not the sort of Halloween "witch" that you might imagine—ugly, pointy black hat, long warty nose, and so on. Instead, like her kingdom Charn she is beautiful, strong, and impressive in such a way that we might mistake it for grandeur or nobility. And when she is transported back to London, she becomes even more so:

> In Charn she had been alarming enough: in London, she was terrifying. . . . But even her height was nothing compared with her beauty, her fierceness, and her wildness. She looked ten times more alive than most of the people one meets in London. (74–75)

But doing something on a grand scale is not the same thing as nobility. It is what might be called the "special effects" view of nobility, but it is mere spectacle. If the

---

*For a bit more background on the concept of the Deplorable Word, remember that C. S. Lewis wrote *The Magician's Nephew* just a few years after the atomic bomb had been invented and used on Japan. It is difficult for many of us today to understand how momentous this event was. In prior generations, war was about having slightly more and bigger weapons than your enemies, but both sides generally had the same types of weapons. And the weapons that existed were very limited in their ability to damage more than a small area at a time. The power of the atomic bomb was on such a different level that many people thought it surely meant the end of the world. It was, in many ways, exactly like a magician discovering the Deplorable Word.

explosions are big enough, we think it is a good movie. If the stadium is large enough, we think the athletes are great. If there are enough lasers and dry ice, we think the band knows how to play. But nobility is a qualitative thing, not a quantitative thing at all.

Even though we might recognize this, notice how Lewis makes us stop short and think about how beautiful, alive, impressive, and grand Jadis is. This may seem like a surprising way for a Christian writer to describe an evil witch, but it is thoroughly biblical. Scripture says that Satan appears as an "angel of light" (2 Cor. 11:14). If Satan looked like some type of Gollum character, or perhaps a cartoon devil complete with a pitchfork, horns, and tail, we might be tempted to laugh or despise him. But if we saw the real thing, Scripture says, we would more likely be tempted to fall down and worship him. Lewis is teaching a very important lesson here: Evil is not always low and despicable; and in fact the most tempting sorts of evil appear on the outside to be beautiful, powerful, liberating, impressive, and noble. We need to be on our guard against evil that looks noble but is not.

## NOBLE ENEMIES

One of the more surprising teachings of the Bible is that we have duties toward our enemies, even enemies in war that we might be trying to kill. Christians are told to love their enemies, yet it is also possible for a Christian to be a soldier and use lethal force. It is pretty obvious that a soldier has duties and responsibilities toward his commander and his comrades, but he also has duties and responsibilities toward his enemies. My father, who served in the Navy for many years, once knew a group of Christian fighter pilots who would hold a prayer meeting before they flew on a mission, and they would always pray for the enemies they were about to fight. They would pray something along the lines of, "Lord, please protect them from us if any of them are being drawn to You or have an interest in spiritual things."

This theme crops up many times in the Narnia stories. A good example is Emeth, the noble Calormene warrior who shows up near the end of *The Last Battle*. All his life, he has been a servant of the false god Tash, but he has always been noble and upright. As the world is ending, he goes through the stable door and finds himself in the final, glorified Narnia—Lewis's vision of heaven—and he meets Aslan, who sets him straight and accepts him as a son. Emeth receives this message joyfully and converts from the worship of Tash to the worship of Aslan. What he says later to the Narnians is interesting:

> "Sir," he said to Peter, "I know not whether you are my friend or my foe, but I should count it my honor to have you for either. Has not one of the poets said that a noble friend is the best gift and a noble enemy the next best?" (183–184)

Though of course we would always prefer to have noble friends, the next best thing is a noble enemy—often because we find that it is much easier to have a noble enemy turn into a friend.

When Peter and Miraz are fighting to the death in *Prince Caspian*, Peter never forgets that he has duties even to the murderous Miraz. When Miraz stumbles and falls, Peter could have just run him through, but his first instinct is to step back and let Miraz get up. The Narnians watching this are initially a bit upset: "Need he be as gentlemanly as that? I suppose he must" (194). Even though Peter is trying to kill Miraz, he has the nobility to make sure it is a fair fight.

Later in *Prince Caspian,* we again see the nobility of the Narnians in the way they treat their Telmarine prisoners. First, they handle them "firmly but without taunts or blows" (210). Although they have complete power over these prisoners (and would have had the right to kill them just hours before in battle), they maintain respect toward them and ensure they keep their dignity. Second, instead of exiling them, Aslan gives them the choice of staying in Narnia and living peacefully alongside the Old Narnians, or returning back to the South Sea islands in our world where they originally came from. So, despite the evils that the Telmarines had done toward the Old Narnians, the latter do not return evil for evil. They win the war, and they accomplish their goal of putting the rightful king (Caspian) on the throne, but then they turn around and give their enemies a fair deal.

Even the most despicable and traitorous enemies must still be fought with nobility. In *The Last Battle,* one of the most memorable scenes is that of the dwarfs betraying Narnia with shouts of "The dwarfs are for the dwarfs!" and then shooting both Calormene soldiers and Narnian horses indiscriminately. It is an unspeakable act.

> It was the Dwarfs who were shooting and—for a moment Jill could hardly believe her eyes—they were shooting the Horses. . . .
> "Little *swine,*" shrieked Eustace, dancing in his rage. "Dirty, filthy, treacherous little brutes." . . .
> But Tirian with his face as stern as stone, said, " . . . And peace, Eustace. Do not scold, like a kitchen-girl. No warrior scolds. Courteous words or else hard knocks are his only language." (138–139)

Lewis, through Tirian, is saying that not only *why* but *how* you fight is important. Whatever your enemy does, they should not be able to drag down your character to their own ignoble level. You must remain noble, and you still have the same duties toward them that you would have toward a more noble enemy.

Although Tirian is the one delivering this rebuke here, earlier in the book he himself failed to treat his enemies nobly. Recall that he and his unicorn Jewel came upon a couple of Calormenes chopping down Narnian forests and using enslaved Narnian horses to do the work for them. When Tirian recognizes what's going on, he and Jewel go into a rage and kill them both on the spot. Having done this, his conscience strikes him:

> "But to leap on them unawares—without defying them— while they were unarmed—faugh! We are two murderers, Jewel. I am dishonored forever." (30)

In other words, he ought to have challenged them first, charged them with their crimes, and either brought them to justice or killed them in a fair fight as an act of war, since they were intruding on Narnian soil. And while this act was not noble, Tirian is a noble king, and so he immediately recognizes and confesses his sin. And not only that—he even surrenders himself to the Calormenes, only to be released later when he calls upon Aslan for help.

It is for similar reasons that Emeth, the noble Calormene, is troubled by his country's war on Narnia. Like Tirian, he knows that you only go to war for just causes, and that you send a formal declaration of war before you attack. Instead, Calormen's army is sneaking and spying its way into Narnia for the simple reason of wanting to take its land and enslave its inhabitants. He says:

> "[A]nd to work by lies and trickery, then my joy depart- ed from me. And most of all when I found we must wait

upon a Monkey, and when it began to be said that Tash and Aslan were one, then the world became dark in my eyes." (185)

So a part of treating enemies nobly is acknowledging that there are rules over both of you, even when you are at war. And you will follow those rules, even if you give up some advantages by doing so. Would it be advantageous to sneak inside a country instead of openly declaring war? Of course. But it would not be noble.

## Nobility and Manners

No discussion on Narnian nobility would be complete without mention of Reepicheep. Not long after Eustace, Edmund, and Lucy board the *Dawn Treader,* Eustace's nasty behavior results in Reepicheep challenging him to a duel. But when Lucy intervenes, Reepicheep reluctantly relents: "'To the convenience of a lady,' said Reepicheep, 'Even a question of honor must give way—at least for the moment'" (17). Now Reepicheep has what some might call an overabundant sense of nobility, in that he is quick to defend (usually with a duel) any good person's honor (quite often his own). But he also knows that courtly manners require that "the convenience of a lady" trump nearly all other concerns.

Now we know that Lewis intentionally gives Reepicheep's character an over-the-top commitment to courtliness and nobility; that is part of what makes him such an enjoyable character. He's an exaggerated cavalier. Recall that during the great battle in *Prince Caspian,* Reepicheep's tail gets cut off and he is gravely wounded. Having been brought before Aslan and healed by Lucy's magic cordial, he yet asks Aslan to restore his tail, arguing that it is a core part of the dignity and honor of a mouse. Aslan responds that perhaps Reepicheep and his people think a bit too much of their own honor. But then he notices that all of Reepicheep's followers are standing behind him with swords drawn. They are ready to cut off their own tails so that Reepicheep will not be alone in his loss. Aslan is much amused by all this, commends them for their "great hearts," and does not pursue the point further, instead granting Reepicheep's request for a restored tail. In all this, Reepicheep is a commendable character, but he and his people—no doubt because of their small size and risk of being taken advantage of—are on the edge of caring too much for their own honor and nobility. So while I do not want to set up Reepicheep as a paragon of nobility that we should all imitate, there are still important lessons underneath.

*The Voyage of the Dawn Treader* offers quite a different example of honor being shown in a social, cultural way. When the ship reaches the "utter East" and must turn back, Aslan reveals to Caspian that Lucy, Edmund, Eustace, and Reepicheep are to go onward to meet Aslan—the children to return to their own world and Reepicheep to fulfill his lifelong destiny. As they are departing, the *Dawn Treader* flies all her flags and puts out all her shields in a formal farewell and display of honor toward them. We tend to think of this type of honor only when there are many people around to see it, like an inauguration parade in Washington, D.C. But here we have King Caspian pulling out all the stops to show honor to four of his friends, all while the ship is alone on the edge of the world. Just like day-to-day manners, these kinds of public ceremonies are ways of *being* noble as well as honoring the nobility of others.

To bring this lesson home in a more practical way, we need to realize that when it comes to showing honor in daily life, the little things matter. Moreover, the heritage of traditional manners in our culture has given us a common language in which to express this honor. For example, the Bible says that when elderly people walk into a room, the younger folks should stand up to acknowledge their presence and show honor to their age. Men, including young men, should learn to do the same for any lady, young or old. These are not just arbitrary rules that have no relevance to modern life, as many of us are tempted to think. Rather, they are a way of recognizing the nobility of others and manifesting the nobility in *ourselves* at the same time. When a man shows this kind of honor to a lady, she is not the only one who receives honor. The man himself is honored as well, because he has demonstrated that he is the kind of man who honors a lady.

For another brief example, let's turn back to *The Horse and His Boy*. At the end of the book, Aravis and Shasta (now Prince Cor) meet again after all their adventures are over, and the formal circumstances of the meeting make it a little awkward:

> The Prince bowed, and a very clumsy bow for a Prince it was. Aravis curtsied in the Calormene style (which is not at all like ours) and did it very well because, of course, she had been taught how. (203)

Cor is just learning how show honor using the manners of Archenland. Having been brought up as a peasant in Calormen, he has no idea how to act among noble people. Notice, though, that he will learn how eventually—as he says, "Education and all sorts of horrible things are going to happen to me" (205). King Lune does not tell him to just "be himself" or "act naturally" or "just forget about all this manners stuff." No, there is real value in practicing the culturally accepted way of giving and receiving honor.

Now compare all the Narnian ways of giving honor to the kind of honor that Calormene royalty receive. Earlier in *The Horse and His Boy* you remember that Aravis and Lasaraleen were sneaking through the old palace and they happened to overhear the Tisroc, prince Rabadash, and the grand vizier making plans for the invasion of Archenland. When the Tisroc enters the room, his two servants are walking backward in front of him, "and of course it is only before royalties that people walk backward" (105). Then I have already talked about how the vizier grovels before the Tisroc and the prince, even allowing himself to be kicked around by them. In Narnia, manners are a way of serving and giving honor to others; in Calormene, manners are a way of exalting oneself at the expense of others. It is a type of false nobility that exists primarily by degrading others—when you cut down all the trees in the forest except one, that last tree looks pretty tall. Lewis shows that the Calormene nobility is fundamentally ignoble.

Just try to imagine a scene where King Peter, King Edmund, Tirian, Caspian, Rilian, or any of the kings of Narnia found someone falling on their face and groveling before them like a beaten dog. Would they enjoy it? Would they find it honorable to themselves? Of course not. They would insist that the person get up and stop making a fool of himself.

At the same time, though, the Narnian type of nobility can still insist on signs of honor and respect. Because there is true authority, true nobility does not have to shrink back and apologize for itself when someone who ought to honor it shows disrespect instead. In *The Voyage of the Dawn Treader,* when Caspian and his group of Narnians arrive with Lord Bern at the house of Gumpas the governor, they find his sentries to be rude, slouching, undisciplined, and sloppily dressed. Lord Bern finally says to one of them,

"Uncover before Narnia, you dog" (54)—in other words, *take off your hat and show some respect.* So, when done with true authority, honor can be demanded as a way of instilling order and discipline. But the honor required of others is never an honor that degrades them.

So Christian manners are a way of giving mutual honor—the giver and receiver are both elevated. Cor bows to Aravis, and Aravis returns the honor with a curtsy. In Calormen, the person who shows honor is degraded and the person who receives honor is puffed up in a grotesque kind of way. You cannot imagine someone bowing to the Tisroc and having the Tisroc return the honor.

## Conclusion

Nobility means dedication, loyalty, humility, and sacrifice—giving yourself away to others. But it also means doing this joyfully and merrily. It is not noble to give yourself away in a sad, gloomy sort of way. There is a type of person who gives himself away while dwelling on how hard and horrible it is for him to do it. But the Bible says that whoever gives also receives. If you lose your life for Jesus' sake, you find it, but if you grasp at your life, you will lose it. So if you give yourself away like a Stoic, because it's the noble thing to do, and you think, "Well, that's it for *my* needs and *my* interests and *my* individuality," then you do not understand this. Because God says that when you give, you receive. This is not to say that you will receive back exactly what you gave up, but it does mean that what you receive will be more glorious and more fulfilling than what you gave up.

Being set free to give and receive is a great cause for gladness and merriment, for breaking out the wine and the fiddlers. That is why Narnia is such a pleasant place. It is also why places like Charn and Calormen are such oppressive places. A handful of people there live in luxury, grasping honor for themselves, while all the rest of the people are poor, oppressed, mistreated, and degraded. Nobility is also not the same thing as power, pride, strength, impressiveness, or grandeur. Jadis and the Tisroc have all these things, but their wickedness shows their nobility to be a sham.

Nobility is something you can show (or not) at any time or any occasion, whether it is special and formal, or just daily life. Your nobility can be tested when you help your mother do the dishes or when you meet the President of the United States. It can be tested on a high school basketball court or a foreign battlefield. Nobility should be practiced everywhere—to your brother, to your mother, to your friends, and to your enemies. The world is a complicated place, but the heart of nobility is simple: sacrifice crowned with joy.

CHAPTER 4

# SPIRITUAL DISCIPLINES

SPIRITUAL DISCIPLINES MAY seem like an odd theme to be getting out of the Narnia stories, so it may require a bit more introduction than the themes of authority, confession, and nobility that we have already covered. By "spiritual disciplines" I mean daily, habitual practices of worship and sanctification. They are a bit like the spiritual equivalent of brushing your teeth—something you do every day so that you no longer think of it as a chore or an annoyance. It is simply something that you know you should do, and are happy to do, because it has real, long-term benefits. You even feel a bit disgusted with yourself for the rest of the day if you happen to forget or not have the chance to do it.

Some good examples of spiritual disciplines are prayer, reading the Bible, going to worship God at church, taking the Lord's Supper, and so on. Theologians call these practices instruments or means of grace that God uses to strengthen you as a Christian, to shape you gradually into a certain kind of person over time.

Now as I said before, this is not the sort of lesson you immediately remember getting out of the Narnia stories. You might remember lessons about bravery and honesty, but not daily Bible reading or prayer. But when you start looking for lessons about the spiritual disciplines in the Narnia stories, you will find them everywhere.

Several of the lessons on this subject are simply things that Lewis says in passing, which you may not notice if you are not paying close attention. For example, in *The Magician's Nephew,* the flying horse Fledge teaches us a very brief lesson on prayer.

> "Well, I *do* think someone might have arranged about our meals," said Digory.
>
> "I'm sure Aslan would have, if you'd asked him," said Fledge.
>
> "Wouldn't he know without being asked?" said Polly.
>
> "I've no doubt he would," said the Horse (still with his mouth full). "But I've a sort of idea he likes to be asked." (163)

This is a question many young Christians wonder about: "If God already knows what we need, why do we need to ask Him for things in prayer?" It is certainly true that God knows what we need before we ask it, but he still wants us to ask, because the act of prayer helps *us* learn something. For example, we learn that we are dependent on God for everything and that He is the one in control of our lives, not ourselves or Mother Nature or some external fate. God knows that this is a very easy lesson for us to forget, so He makes sure we relearn it every day in the form of prayer.

Also in *The Magician's Nephew,* Lewis makes a passing comment on the value of repetitive lessons on the basics of Scripture, such as the Ten Commandments. When Digory enters the mountain garden to pluck a magical golden apple and bring it back to Aslan, Jadis tempts him to take the apple for himself and achieve immortality. The temptation is very strong, but one of the reasons he does not fall for it is that "Things like Do Not Steal were, I think, hammered into boys' heads a good deal harder in those days than they are now" (173–174). Now Digory might have rolled his eyes when being taught to memorize "Do not steal" for the hundredth time, but what he did not realize was that the lesson was becoming an automatic part of his character. So when he reaches a moment of crisis, this habitual spiritual discipline in his upbringing was able to kick in and help him resist the temptation.

## Following the Signs: *The Silver Chair*

In the two examples above, Lewis is just throwing a brief lesson into the story, almost in passing. And I think this is how specific lessons on the spiritual disciplines appear in most of the Narnia books. But I would argue that in *The Silver Chair* the spiritual disciplines are actually a central theme of the story, and accordingly we will be spending most of our time in this chapter on that particular book.

### THE SIGNS: MEMORY AND FORGETFULNESS

You will remember how Eustace and Jill enter Aslan's country at the beginning of the book, and how they become separated when Jill's foolishness causes Eustace to fall off a huge cliff, though Aslan appears at just the right moment and sends Eustace safely to Narnia ahead of her. Then Aslan meets with Jill and gives her the task of finding Prince Rilian, along with the signs which he will use to guide her and Eustace on the quest. It is clear that Aslan wants to impress upon her the great importance of the signs. He makes her repeat them over and over until she has them completely memorized. He tells her:

But, first, remember, remember, remember the signs. Say them to yourself when you wake in the morning and when you lie down at night, and when you wake in the middle of the night. (27)

The exhortation to *remember* is a very biblical lesson. Aslan's language in this passage has strong echoes of what God tells Israel to do in Deuteronomy 6:6–9:

And these words, which I command thee this day, shall be in thine heart: And thou shalt teach them diligently unto thy children, and shalt talk of them when thou sittest in thine house, and when thou walkest by the way, and when thou liest down, and when thou risest up. And thou shalt bind them for a sign upon thine hand, and they shall be as frontlets between thine eyes. And thou shalt write them upon the posts of thy house, and on thy gates.

Meditating on God's word should be an activity that permeates your whole day, even filling in those little spaces of free time that you get when you are walking down the street. Think of God's words when you wake up in the morning and when you are going to sleep. Repeat them. Memorize them. They are the signs by which God guides you through the confusion of the world, and without them you are lost.

So God says that remembering is a fundamental duty. This means that forgetting is a sin, which makes it all the more strange that we often try to turn forgetfulness into an *excuse* for sin. Have you ever tried to excuse yourself in front of your parents by saying, "Sorry, I forgot"? They told you to clean your room, or rake the yard, or weed the garden, or stop leaving your dirty socks on the couch, and for whatever reason you failed to obey. You may have genuinely forgotten, but that doesn't matter. So in this situation your parents ought to respond, "Well, thank you for confessing the additional sin of forgetting. And there will be extra discipline for that. Not obeying was bad enough, but forgetting makes things worse." It is no good for you to say (or think), "But wait—forgetting is supposed to be an excuse!" because it is not. Remembering to obey is itself an essential part of obedience; you cannot separate the two.

## THE FIRST SIGN

Before Aslan sends Jill off to Narnia, he gives her an interesting bit of advice: While she is up in Aslan's country everything seems perfectly clear, but down in the daily world of Narnia things are going to be more muddled and confused. Appearances may be deceiving:

> And the signs which you have learned here will not look at all as you expect them to look, when you meet them there. That is why it is so important to know them by heart and pay no attention to appearances. Remember the signs and believe the signs. Nothing else matters. (27)

This is one of the main reasons why Aslan wants Jill to have the signs absolutely memorized, to the point where it takes no mental effort to call them up. Because the real world is a confusing place and the signs may not be what they first seem, Jill cannot be trying to remember a sign and trying to recognize the fulfillment of the sign at the same time. The signs need to become second nature if they are to be effective guides.

Lewis is teaching a similar lesson about spiritual disciplines. When you are doing your daily devotions, or listening to the sermon in church, or participating in a Bible study, God's message seems very clear: trust in Christ, do not steal, honor your parents, forgive seventy times seven, do not commit adultery, and so on. But real life, daily life, tends to make your choices *seem* much messier and more complicated, and the mind has a way of trying to actively forget and ignore what God says about a certain sin while the temptation is working. Spiritual disciplines prepare you to resist this tendency.

Despite Aslan's warning to always remember the signs and not be deceived by appearances, Jill finds that it is all too easy for things to go wrong. Aslan blows her across the sea to Narnia, and although she arrives just moments after Eustace, she is distracted by the spectacle of a great royal procession and forgets to tell him the first sign right away. The first sign was that Eustace would see an old friend and that he should greet him immediately in order to get help for their quest. It turns out that this old friend is King Caspian himself, who was a young man when he knew Eustace but now is very old and near death. He is also just departing on a final sea voyage to the east, and the great procession is his final farewell ceremony. When Jill finally realizes all this, it is too late and Caspian has already departed. Her response?

> "Oh, shut up," said Jill impatiently. "It's far worse than you think. We've muffed the first Sign." Of course, [Eustace] Scrubb did not understand this. (45)

So before Eustace even knows what is going on, Jill has "muffed" the first sign. Now, at first this looks like an honest mistake. After all, who wouldn't have been distracted by the great farewell procession? And how could Jill have known that Eustace would not be able to recognize his old friend? But deeper down, the issue is simple. Jill fails to obey. She fails to keep the signs foremost in her mind, and she fails to heed Aslan's warning to not be fooled by appearances. In the end, there are no excuses, and Jill clearly has a lot to learn about the discipline of the signs.

## The Second Sign

Fortunately, Aslan does not allow Jill's mistakes with the first sign to end the quest then and there. Jill and Eustace still get some help (though much less, and in a much different form than they might have otherwise), and they eventually meet up with Puddleglum the Marsh-wiggle to begin their mission in earnest. If you are not familiar with the story, Puddleglum is a character who has a comically dour and gloomy exterior, but he turns out to be quite useful, fiercely loyal, and suspicious about the world in all the right ways.

Jill tells him about the signs—the second sign is that they should travel to the North and seek the ruined city of the giants—and they begin their quest to the north, meeting all kinds of hardships along the way, until Jill and Eustace have had just about enough of adventures. Winter is coming fast, and they have just barely escaped the flying boulders of some very rowdy giants when they meet a green lady riding with a silent, black knight (whom they discover, much later, to be none other than the evil enchantress and the lost prince they are seeking). The green lady tells them to stop at Harfang, the home of the "gentle giants," to get some shelter, rest, good food, warm baths, and all the other comforts they have been missing for the past several weeks. She even tells them that if they hurry they will be in time for the autumn festival.

They really ought to be suspicious of this, but instead it becomes the only goal that Jill and Eustace can think about. The quest, the prince, and the signs are forgotten with the promise of warmth, feasting, and comfort. Only Puddleglum is suspicious: "anyway, Aslan's signs had said

nothing about staying with giants, gentle or otherwise"
(91–92). This is a key point. Puddleglum does not just
think of the signs as random things that will happen which
they need to be able to recognize. The signs are not just
about being able to react to something after it happens.
Instead, he argues that they ought to be using the signs
themselves in all their decision making, to guide them in
what steps to take next.

Aslan had told Jill to *remember, remember, remember*
the signs. But after the green lady tells them about Harfang, all they can do is *forget, forget, forget.*

> They never talked about Aslan, or even about the lost
> prince, now. And Jill gave up her habit of repeating the
> signs over to herself every night and morning. (92–93)

They stop thinking about the signs and their quest and
start thinking only about the comforts they will have at
Harfang. Now this slow process of disobedience has an
interesting effect: it makes them feel more sorry for themselves, more grumpy, more selfish, and more snappy with
each other and Puddleglum. When they were first going
into the wilderness to find a lost prince with no promise
of comfort or baths or good food, they were cheerful and
happy. They were repeating the signs, obeying Aslan, and
roughing it—joyfully. But when they start being disobedient and actively seeking comfort instead of obedience, it
immediately starts making them miserable.

The same thing is true of the spiritual disciplines. If you
stop reading your Bible, saying your prayers, and worshiping with a whole heart on the Lord's day, you will eventually start to see the effects of that. And when you have been
coasting along for a while, you will surprise yourself by
suddenly breaking out in anger, quarreling with your siblings, disobeying parents, putting yourself ahead of others.

If you become lax in your disciplines because you want to fill up your time with something more "fun," then you will quickly find yourself to be more miserable. There is a direct connection between lack of spiritual discipline and lack of both joy and spiritual fruit in your life.

So, at last the travelers catch sight of Harfang in the distance. But as they are making their way toward it, they get caught in a blinding snowstorm and have to work their way over some strange, difficult ground. There are small cliffs, strange dead-end trenches, and odd smokestack-like rocks around them. If they had been paying more attention to the signs, they might have recognized that they were in the ruins of the ancient giants' city—which is the second sign. However, she and Eustace are too consumed with thoughts of Harfang to be paying any attention to the signs or their own surroundings. Puddleglum is again the only one who keeps his head and continues to be faithful:

> "Are you still sure of those signs, [Jill] Pole? What's the one we ought to be after now?"
>
> "Oh, come *on!* Bother the signs," said Pole. "Something about someone mentioning Aslan's name, I think. But I'm jolly well not going to give a recitation here."
>
> As you see, she had gotten the order wrong. That was because she had given up saying the signs over every night. (101)

Of course Jill has gotten the order wrong; that was the fourth sign, and she should have been searching for the second. Because she has given up repeating the signs, and replaced them in her mind with thoughts of her own comfort, she fails to recognize the fulfillment of the sign. And not only that, when Puddleglum tries to bring her back into obedience, she snaps at him. She knows he is right, but she is so deep in her own disobedient thoughts that she shuts out that thought with a "bother the signs."

## The Third Sign

So the travelers are initially welcomed by the "gentle" giants at Harfang, and at first they seem to get what they want—good food, baths, and comfortable beds. But the first night there, Aslan appears to Jill in a dream and shows her the ruins of a giant city in the plain below Harfang, with the giant words "UNDER ME" visible on some of the paving stones. And when Jill wakes up, she and the others see that the city and the words are really there. They realize that the letters of this inscription were the same strange trenches they had climbed through in the snowstorm on their way to Harfang. If they had been paying attention to the signs all along, they would have realized this and would have been well on their way to the end of their quest, instead of being stuck in the giants' castle. As Puddleglum points out,

> "We'd have got down under those paving-stones somehow or other. Aslan's instructions always work: there are no exceptions. But how to do it *now*—that's another matter." (120–121)

Soon enough, they discover the awful truth about Harfang: that their hosts (and the green lady) are treacherous. The giants plan to put them all into a "man pie" and eat them at the giants' Autumn Festival. They plot a way to escape as soon as they can, but the giants catch sight of them and start following them toward the ruined city. In a last-ditch attempt to escape, they hide under a projecting rock, only to fall down a steep slope and find themselves deep underground with no light, no food, and no water. But as Puddleglum says, "We're back on the right lines.

We were to go under the Ruined City and we *are* under it. We're following the instructions again" (148). Even though they initially missed the sign through disobedience, Aslan in his kindness and grace allows them to get back on track and resume where they ought to have been.

## THE FINAL SIGN

The final sign—that when the first person in their travels tells them to do something in Aslan's name, they are to do it—is also the only sign they manage to get right on the first try. I have already discussed this scene at length in chapter one, so we can skip some of the story line and get right to the primary lesson here. When the prince calls on them in the name of Aslan to release him from the silver chair, the children and the Marsh-wiggle have a very simple choice. He is giving them the sign, even though it does not appear to be the right circumstances for the sign; they think the prince is in a fit of lunacy. Is the sign still the sign if it comes out of the mouth of a lunatic? Did Aslan really want them to do something that appears to mean certain death at that lunatic's hands?

But "on the other hand, what had been the use of learning the signs if they weren't going to obey them?" And "Aslan didn't tell Pole what would happen. He only told her what to do" (167). To their credit, they all decide to trust Aslan and release the prince, which of course breaks his enchantment and sets the stage for them to kill the enchantress, foil her plans to invade Narnia with an army of Earthmen, and finally return home.

After the close call at Harfang, they all began to take the final sign very seriously, which in turn allowed them to make this final snap decision that turns the whole tide of the story. The spiritual disciplines work the same way; they build you up gradually over time so that when the time comes to make a difficult decision, you have a strong foundation to make the right choice.

## False Disciplines

Just as in previous chapters I have talked about true and false authority, true and false confession, and true and false nobility, so also there are true and false disciplines. If you know your way around your Bible and your church history, this lesson is nothing new—for every act of real, joyful piety and discipline there are many, many temptations toward dour, soul-killing asceticism and legalism.

Take the example of Nikabrik in *Prince Caspian*. Nikabrik has a harsh character and follows a harsh way of life. Lewis goes out of his way to point this out. Trumpkin enjoys a good pipe, but Nikabrik is not a smoker. When all the other Narnians gather to dance on the great dancing lawn, Nikabrik does not join in. He does not play an instrument or even stomp, clap, sing, or shout. "Only Nikabrik stayed where he was, looking on in silence" (82). In other words, Lewis is saying that there is a certain type of wickedness that is a dour killjoy. We typically think of wickedness as always self-indulgent, always trying to break the rules in order to have fun, always seeking pleasure. Lewis reminds us that quite often the opposite is true: The wicked look down with pinched faces at all the righteous people having a good time. Spiritual disciplines should make you joyful; they are not to be confused with harsh asceticism or dead legalism.

We see the same kind of situation with Eustace's parents in *The Voyage of the Dawn Treader*. Lewis goes out of his way to describe them as vegetarians, non-smokers, and teetotalers who wear "a special kind of underclothes" (3). They encourage Eustace to read dry nonfiction books and they disapprove of fairy stories, imagination, and creativity. So they certainly have disciplined and ordered lives, but what does it do for them? It is a killjoy kind of discipline, and it makes Eustace into a brat—or, as the English would say, a "rotter."

A final illustration of this comes from *The Lion, the Witch and the Wardrobe* and is also one of my favorite passages in all the Narnia stories. It happens late in the story when Aslan is "on the move" and the White Witch's spell of eternal winter is starting to fall apart. And the witch comes upon a group of creatures in the forest who are enjoying a Christmas banquet given to them by Father Christmas himself—who had been, as you know, unable to enter Narnia during all the years of the witch's reign. So when the witch sees this feast she is furious:

> "Speak, vermin!" she said again. "Or do you want my dwarf to find you a tongue with his whip? What is the meaning of all this gluttony, this waste, this self-indulgence? Where did you get all these things?" (115)

Lewis is teaching us the difference between a discipline of joy and a discipline of harsh denial. Aslan has the discipline of joy, symbolized by his bringing springtime, but the witch has the discipline of denial, symbolized by her hundred years of winter.

Now Lewis is *not* saying that following Aslan is always easy and fun, or that following the witch will never get you any pleasure. Both sides have pleasures and hardships, but Aslan puts them in the right order while the witch puts them in the wrong order. Aslan's ways give lasting and deep joy through (and following) temporary hardship, while the witch's ways give long-lasting hardships that result from short-lived and shallow pleasures. Edmund starts by taking the Turkish Delight from the witch but ends up as her slave. Jill and Eustace endure many hardships to find Prince Rilian, but at the end they break out from the underground tunnel into the wild Narnian snow dance. In the same way, God sends us trials in order to grow us into maturity, so that we can have the capacity for much greater joy. But the devil wants to give you brief pleasure now in exchange for sorrows later.

There is another kind of false discipline that is actually an improper attitude toward true discipline. This attitude accepts the right kind of godly, spiritual disciplines, but it misses the whole point of the discipline. It wants the discipline for its own sake, rather than for the goals for which God intended it. Eustace, pre-conversion, is a good example of this. Lewis is describing what kind of a student he is:

> [F]or though he didn't care much about any subject for his own sake, he cared a great deal about marks [grades] and would even go to people and say, "I got so much. What did you get?" (30)

Eustace is not the type of student who gets his test or essay back from the teacher and thinks, "Look at what I've learned—and I can learn more from my mistakes." Instead, he turns to his classmates and says, "I got a 92—what did you get?" on the assumption, of course, that the other person probably scored lower. This type of student accepts the discipline of study but forgets that its purpose is *learning something,* not puffing up your pride by comparing yourself to others or trying to take others down a notch.

Ask any teacher or homeschooling parent, and they will tell you the question they most hate to hear from their students: "Will this be on the test?" They do not like hearing it because it shows that the student will only accept the discipline of study for a very narrow and shallow set of reasons—doing well enough on the test to get approval from their parents and peers.

Another type of joyless discipline is the fussy, bureaucratic dictatorship of Gumpas, the governor of the Lone Islands in *The Voyage of the Dawn Treader.* Gumpas loves to be self-important. He loves to act busy, have a tight schedule, and deny audience to his subjects. He loves shuffling papers and putting his official seal on everything. But this false bureaucratic discipline misses the entire point of government, just as Eustace misses the entire point of schooling. Caspian swiftly deals with this problem by acting very *un*disciplined:

> They lifted [the table], and flung it on one side of the hall where it rolled over, scattering a cascade of letters, dossiers, inkpots, pens, sealing-wax and documents. (56)

To Gumpas, this type of behavior is that of an anarchist or rebel. But he is missing the point and Caspian is not at all out of line. Caspian needs to purge the government of Gumpas's false discipline in order to clear the way for a government that delivers real discipline and real justice.

## Disciplines and Pleasure: Two Tables

The Bible teaches that everyone will end up eating at one of two tables: the table of demons or the table of the Lord (1 Cor. 10:21). Lewis teaches the same lesson in the Narnia stories: there is the table of Aslan against the table of Aslan's enemies. In *The Voyage of the Dawn Treader,* when the ship arrives on Ramandu's island near the edge of the world, they find a table set by Aslan:

> There were flagons of gold and silver and curiously-wrought glass; and the smell of the fruit and the wine blew towards them like a promise of all happiness. (193)

Another example is the rich, beautiful mountain garden that Digory travels to in *The Magician's Nephew.* Aslan's table is not harsh, forbidding, or miserly. It is an abundant, joyful feast, "the promise of all happiness."

Perhaps the clearest manifestation of the table of demons is the White Witch's Turkish Delight in *The Lion, the Witch and the Wardrobe.* Not long after she has met Edmund, she asks "What would you like best to eat?" and Edmund requests the Turkish Delight. The problem with the witch's food is not that it is cheap or poor-tasting; rather, "Edmund had never tasted anything more delicious." But if Aslan's table and the witch's table both provide pleasures, what is the difference between them? First of all, the witch's food—although it is initially sweet—does not satisfy.

> [T]he more he ate the more he wanted to eat, and he never asked himself why the Queen should be so inquisitive. . . .
> [The witch] knew, though Edmund did not, that this was enchanted Turkish Delight and that anyone who had once tasted it would want more and more of it, and would even, if they were allowed, go on eating it till they killed themselves. (37–38)

The witch's food is not satisfying. The more he gets, the more he wants, and he is never happy or contented with what he has. It turns into an addiction that replaces the desire for wholesome food, but never satisfies hunger or nourishes the body. In the end, it leads straight to death.

Second, the witch's food tries to give immediate gratification; she has hardly met Edmund when she says that she will give him whatever he likes best. Aslan's table, on the other hand, awaits those who have put in a lifetime of faithful service. Aslan does not simply meet someone for the first time and give them all their heart's desire. Not only would that be bad for people spiritually, it would also be a very poor adventure story: *Edmund went into Narnia and Aslan gave him a wonderful banquet. The End.* God tells a much better story than that, and that is the story that Lewis is imitating. Aslan teaches his followers to be faithful over time, through hardships and temptation, rough times and smooth, until they are mature enough to come in the end to a place that has "the promise of all happiness." Of course this does not mean that God denies us all pleasures until heaven—certainly he does offer real blessings and times of rest along the way. But God's table is not fully revealed until the end.

If you eat the devil's candy, it's going to be sweet, but all you have afterwards are sticky fingers, an ill stomach, and—in a short time—the gnawing desire for more. No matter how many times you eat and are dissatisfied, you will never get enough. The most in-your-face examples of this in the real world are drug and alcohol addiction. Addicts start out having a little, then want more and more until they cannot control the desire. It leaves them miserable and dissatisfied every time but they keep going back to it. It replaces the desire for healthy pleasures, wholesome food, friendships, and work. They might be able to convince themselves that they are "living it up," but the end of that road is spiritual and physical death.

That is the devil's (and the White Witch's) way of doing things. God (and Aslan's) ways are the opposite. God wants us to work now, resist temptation, be faithful, and practice moderation. He wants us to sacrifice for others, putting them ahead of ourselves. He wants us to give up our lives to gain them, to die in order to rise again to more glorious life.

Now it is all too easy to imagine that we only need to do this in the "big things" but may conveniently ignore it in our minor day-to-day decisions. But this lesson of "death and resurrection" for the vast majority of young Christians is not about literally taking a bullet for someone, or even resisting a major temptation like adultery or drug addiction. Remember that those who are faithful in little will be faithful in much. Suppose you get some Christmas or birthday money and it is burning a hole in your pocket. You want to go out to the mall immediately and spend it all. You don't feel like saving or tithing any of it. It seems like a trivial issue, but is that attitude molding you in the direction of the Lord's table? No—it's Edmund and the Turkish Delight. Even in such a small-seeming decision, you are taking the first steps on a long road toward one of two very different destinations.

# Disciplines, Grace, and Forgiveness

As you begin to seriously pursue the spiritual disciplines, you will sooner or later discover why they are called *disciplines*. They are difficult, and you will fail in many ways. Because of this, it is important to remember two things: that God is quick to forgive and quick to give us the ability to follow him more faithfully. He is not using these disciplines to crush us. They are grace, not law.

Remember that in *The Silver Chair,* Jill and Eustace "muffed" all the signs but one. The adventure could have been over after each time they made a mistake, but Aslan forgave them and allowed them to keep going. Now at least Jill and Eustace got the final sign right—but what about those who seem to have gotten *all* the signs wrong?

Can people like that still be saved? Lewis gives several clues to his thinking in *The Last Battle*. When Aslan is judging all the creatures at the end of the story, they stand before him one by one and look into his face. Then they either recognize Aslan (and He them) and joyfully enter into the new, glorified Narnia, or their faces show their hatred for Aslan and they depart off into the darkness. In describing this, Lewis includes a few interesting details:

> There were some queer specimens among them. Eustace even recognized one of those very Dwarfs who had helped to shoot the Horses. But he had no time to wonder about that sort of thing (and anyway it was no business of his) for a great joy put everything else out of his head. (176)

The shooting of the horses in this book is one of the most awful scenes in all of the stories, and this dwarf had been part of this atrocity at the end of his life. If Aslan had given him "signs" to follow, he had muffed the last and probably most important one. Yet in the end, he can still be forgiven and remain a servant of Aslan. At this point, we as readers are so angry with the dwarfs that we would like to see them all roundly punished, but that is not how Aslan does things. Lewis is showing us that there is always forgiveness and grace with God. The dwarf is saved by grace, not condemned by his works. Note too that Aslan's followers do not have time to judge one another or question Aslan's judgment about things that are none of their business—the joy is too great to worry about things like that.

This is a thoroughly biblical lesson. Yes, we are supposed to "follow the signs": do good works, pray regularly, read God's Word, and worship God in spirit and truth. But in the end we are not saved because we have always worked hard to be good little Christians; we are saved by grace through faith. Spiritual disciplines are God's way of blessing us and leading us into strength and maturity. They are not His way of burdening us with guilt. He has saved us *from* guilt, so why would He want to give us more of it?

# The Reward of Discipline

We have already talked about the rewards of discipline, and that Aslan's way is to bring his servants through hardships and reward them richly in the end. But there is another aspect to the rewards of discipline that is much more unexpected—and a bit disconcerting to those who are just starting out on their spiritual journey. This lesson is that, quite often, *the reward of discipline is more difficult discipline.*

What happens when a child finishes first grade? His parents and teachers congratulate him on all his hard work, and then they put him in second grade where he will have to work harder. And this process repeats for another eleven, or fifteen, or more years. And when he finally graduates? He will find a career, a spouse, a household, and children waiting for him—all things that require more discipline (but also offer richer returns) than his schooling.

I vividly remember learning this lesson in my own life. I grew up in a family that was not at all mechanically-minded. Our family was all about books, history, literature, and all the liberal arts—not engineering. Then I joined the Navy and entered submarine school. The week before it started I got a glimpse of one of our textbooks, and it was all about machinery, valves, the physics of water pressure, and that sort of thing, which to me was like a foreign language. I remember thinking, "I can't possibly do this." I had completed one stage of my life—one set of disciplines—but then I was handed something much harder. And I had to simply buckle down and complete those disciplines as well. It was not easy, but it was what God had set before me.

So you should not be trying to reach some stage of your life where you can just sit on your laurels, enjoy the view, and tell God, "Okay, now you can leave me alone." Those who faithfully finish the tasks God has given them right now will always have the opportunity to take on bigger and better tasks. That is God's way.

Shasta learns this lesson near the end of *The Horse and His Boy*. He has crossed the great desert, outrun Rabadash's forces, and been chased by a great lion which, unbeknownst to Shasta and Aravis, was Aslan Himself forcing them to make the final push. Shasta even jumps off his horse to run back and confront Aslan, thinking He was an ordinary lion about to kill Aravis and Hwin. Finally, they reach the hermit's enclosure and collapse exhausted. Now what does Shasta learn? Does the hermit say, "Congratulations, you've been very brave and endured many hardships. Have a hot meal and a bed"? Quite the opposite:

> "If you run now, without a moment's rest, you will still be in time to warn King Lune."
> Shasta's heart fainted at these words for he felt he had no strength left. And he writhed inside at what seemed the cruelty and unfairness of the demand. He had not yet learned that if you do one good deed your reward usually is to be set to do another and harder and better one. But all he said out loud was:
> "Where is the King?" (145–146)

Shasta has done well and he is tired. But the hardest part of his journey is still ahead—now he has to run on foot to warn King Lune before the Calormene invaders reach his castle. And after Shasta completes this task as well? He receives the next challenge when he learns that he is really King Lune's lost son and thus will be the next king of Archenland: "Education and other horrible things are going to happen to me" (205). And when he completes his education and becomes king, what then? "For this is what it means to be a king: to be first in every desperate attack and last in every desperate retreat" (223).

The fact that Shasta receives harder tasks as fast as he completes them is not a sad thing. Shasta grew up in a poor fisherman's hut, and if Aslan had not had great plans for him, he could have stayed a peasant the rest of his life and never had any adventures or faced any challenges. But Aslan led him on a more difficult path, a path that led him to the throne of Archenland. It is a wonderful and joyful thing.

This is how God calls us up into maturity. When you finish one grade at school, you should be proud of that and happy that God has called you to the next higher grade, where you will work more and learn more. It does not at first make sense to us that the reward of discipline is more discipline. Many of God's ways do not make sense at first. I doubt it immediately made sense to Adam that he had to bury grain in the ground in order to get more grain. You do one good deed, and God says, "Good job, here's a harder and a better deed." This is God's way, and it is a way of *blessing*.

## Don't Keep Digging Up the Seed

When kids are in kindergarten, one of their first science projects always seems to be to fill an egg or milk carton with dirt, plant some beans in it, and watch them as they sprout and grow. Now four- and five-year-olds tend to be impatient, so invariably they want to dig up the bean every few hours to see how it is doing. They might do this on and off for a couple of days and come to the conclusion that the bean is not growing and is *never* going to grow. The problem is that of course the bean is not going to do well when it keeps getting dug up.

To conclude this chapter I want to give one bit of practical advice for taking on the spiritual disciplines in your life: *don't keep digging up the seed.* When you start practicing the spiritual disciplines on a regular basis, your temptation is to keep peering inside your heart every day, looking for signs of growth. When you do not immediately see any, and when you feel like you keep falling into the same sins and temptations every week, you might be tempted to think that the disciplines are not doing you any good at all. You say your prayers twice a day, you read God's Word, you go to church and take communion, but you cannot feel yourself growing.

At these times you need to have faith, because you *are* growing. The things you are doing and learning are shaping you and settling down deep into your heart and mind. If you are growing up this way, living faithfully in a faithful family and community, you need to realize what an enormous blessing and advantage it is. When someone becomes a Christian as an adult, they have to start relearning many of the things they ought to have learned as children. Even when they work hard to learn a particular lesson, they might know it only in their head, but not in their heart, and they have trouble applying it in all parts of their lives. But Christians who grow up in the faith learn these lessons so deep in their bones that they are almost instincts, and so deep that they have even forgotten how they learned them. A child does not know how he learned his native language, and he does not ever notice his progress while he is learning it. But in a few short years he is fluent—a native speaker—and the envy of anyone who has to learn that language *after* they have become an adult, when it is much harder. This is the value of "following the signs" in your life, of doing the same things every morning, every night, every Lord's day.

The next time you read *The Silver Chair,* think about the signs as the spiritual disciplines you are trying to keep in your own life—prayer, studying the Word, worshiping God, putting His kingdom ahead of the cares of this life. And rejoice in the disciplines, even when they do not seem to be having any immediate effect. It is working. Follow it through and trust God, because He will bless you.

# CHAPTER 5

# ℒOVE OF STORY

As we have been talking about various "lessons" that we can take away from the Chronicles of Narnia, I have wanted to be careful that I did not wreck the stories by making sure that everybody only gets Edified, with a capital *E* of course. The Narnia stories are *stories,* after all, and I wholeheartedly encourage you to simply enjoy them on that level, without getting all worked up about making sure you are learning all the lessons that you think you are supposed to be learning from them.

But at the same time, C. S. Lewis knew that stories *instruct,* and he was not shy about doing that. He was not even shy about using his stories to teach that lesson about stories. In a number of places, the stories are in fact *stories about stories.* In other words, the Narnia stories don't just instruct us about topics like authority, nobility, confession, and so on; they also teach about how stories themselves work and how we ought to think about them. Over and over, Lewis uses his stories to teach us that stories prepare people to live well in their own story—the story of your life. Consequently, it is vital not only that people read stories, but that they also read the right *kind* of stories.

# The Importance of Story

In *The Horse and His Boy,* Lewis has an apt comparison between English and Calormene education:

> For in Calormen, storytelling (whether the stories are true or made up) is a thing you're taught, just as English boys and girls are taught essay writing. The difference is that people want to hear the stories, whereas I never heard of anyone who wanted to read the essays. (35)

We live in a time and a culture that extols nonfiction over fiction. Stories may be good for the occasional entertainment in order to help us unwind, but that is all. They are optional fluff, like eating dessert. According to many thinkers today, in order for a piece of writing to be *really* important, it has to be purely factual, dry, and boring. For example, we teach history the way it was taught under Miraz:

> The sort of "History" that was taught in Narnia under Miraz's rule was duller than the truest history you ever read and less true than the most exciting adventure story. (*Prince Caspian,* 199)

In Lewis's time, and still today, far too many people (especially self-styled intellectuals) think that exciting stories are just for children, and if you want something that is really true and useful, it has to be lectured in a boring way by adults with long faces.

Now this does not mean that Lewis wanted to go the opposite way and convince us that nonfiction is unimportant. Rather, he wants to show us where the balance lies. C. S. Lewis was one of the great scholars of the twentieth century, and as a scholar he wrote a good deal of academic nonfiction. But one of the reasons he was such a great scholar is that he understood the limitations of scholarship and the kinds of handicaps that scholars frequently labor under. Many kinds of truth can be communicated much better through stories. For Lewis, the right kind of adventure story is full of truth, while the worst kind of history is full of lies (and dull to boot). Lewis wanted to restore our trust in the ability of stories to communicate truth.

As Caspian says to the Pevensie children, who were once legendary kings and queens of Narnia:

> "Sometimes I did wonder if there really was such a person as Aslan: but then sometimes I wondered if there were really people like you. Yet there you are." (70)

## Stories as Preparation

One of the most important lessons that Lewis teaches is that knowing the right stories is good preparation. In the case of the Pevensie children, their knowledge of the right sorts of stories prepares them for their experiences in Narnia. When they find themselves in an unfamiliar or daunting situation, the first thing they think about is, "What would someone in this kind of story do?"

When the children are pulled back into Narnia at the beginning of *Prince Caspian,* they find themselves on a deserted island covered with a dense forest. They have no idea where they are, why they have been brought back, what they are supposed to do next, or even how they are going to get their next meal. Now, since they come from a family that values good stories, their first instinct is to think about the stories they have read:

> "It's like being shipwrecked," remarked Edmund. "In the books they always find springs of clear, fresh water on the island. We'd better go and look for them." (6)

"Look here. There's only one thing to be done. We must explore the wood. Hermits and knights-errant and people like that always manage to live somehow if they're in a forest. They find roots and berries and things." (11)

In *The Voyage of the Dawn Treader*, they come upon a strange island with a small lake. There is some discarded armor nearby and a life-size golden statue of a man in a diving position at the bottom of the lake. Lewis, showing some good humor, writes about how Edmund's reading habits come in handy to help them piece together the clues and figure out what has happened: "Edmund, the only one of the party who had read several detective stories, had meanwhile been thinking" (124).

Later on in the same story, Caspian lands on an island where three of the lords he seeks are in an enchanted sleep. He learns from Ramandu, the caretaker of the island, and his daughter that the enchantment will not be broken until someone sails to the utter East—the edge of the world. Caspian immediately falls in love with Ramandu's daughter (we learn later in *The Silver Chair* that she is his future bride), and he draws on the commonplaces of fairy tales to frame his situation (and give a little hint to Ramandu's daughter):

"And what are we to do about the Sleepers?" asked Caspian. "In the world from which my friends come" (here he nodded at Eustace and the Pevensies) "they have a story of a prince or a king coming to a castle where all the people lay in an enchanted sleep. In that story he could not dissolve the enchantment until he had kissed the Princess."

"But here," said the girl, "it is different. Here he cannot kiss the Princess till he has dissolved the enchantment." (202–203)

Throughout *The Voyage of the Dawn Treader,* Eustace is the prime example of someone who has *not* read the right kind of stories. When his bad behavior prompts threats of "getting two dozen" he has no idea that it is a sailors' term for being tied to the mast and getting two dozen lashes: "I didn't know what this meant until Edmund explained it to me. It comes in the sort of books the Pevensie kids read" (74). Eustace would never have read any sort of maritime adventure story that involved sailors getting flogged; his parents would not have allowed him near one. We'll talk more about Eustace's reading in a moment, but for now it is enough to point out that Lewis highlights the big differences between him and the Pevensies at least partly in terms of the type of the books that they read.

The examples above are good examples of how Lewis's passing comments highlight the fact that our daily lives are permeated by stories, whether we know it or not. Many of our instinctive reactions, attitudes, character traits, decisions, and the ways we frame our experiences are influenced by what we have spent our time reading (or, in the case of modern readers, also *watching*). The above examples are fairly trivial, but the same is true for all the important lessons we have covered in the previous chapters. Lessons on authority, confession, nobility, and spiritual disciplines are best learned by experience, example, and imitation, not by reading a twelve-step self-help guide. But if someone has not grown up around good examples of authority or confession or nobility—and many, many people in our modern American culture have not and are still not—how are they to learn about them? The next best way is to learn them through stories.

This is how Reepicheep got the character and attitude that he has: "For his mind was full of forlorn hopes, death-or-glory charges, and last stands" (67). Reepicheep would have done wonderfully at the Alamo—that was his kind of battle. If anyone had told him about the Alamo, or any other hopeless cause (provided of course that it was noble), he would have loved hearing the story. He thrives on that sort of thing. Now, as I've already said, Reepicheep is an intentionally exaggerated character, but he is a great example of how someone's character can be shaped by story. And if you really want to have nobility or learn true authority in real life, stories are one of the primary ways of doing that. Stories give you examples of the type of person you want to become, and they help you to grow up into that sort of character and take on that frame of mind. Stories shape how you think, for good or ill.

We have already discussed how Lewis draws contrasts between Narnia and Calormen based on the way their cultures treat stories. Lewis says Narnian poetry is better than Calormene poetry because it is passionate and stirring, while Calormenes write poetry about useful bits of advice: "Aravis and Cor prepared themselves to be bored, for the only poetry they knew was the Calormene kind" (*The Horse and His Boy*, 221). If a Calormene poet were transported to our world, he would probably write a few lines about changing your oil every three thousand miles and rotating your tires. As one Calormene says, "For the gods have withheld from the barbarians [the Narnians] the light of discretion as that their poetry is not, like ours, full of choice apophthegms and useful maxims, but it is all of love and war" (117). Of course Lewis also notes that Calormenes were very good at non-poetic storytelling, because it was a crucial part of their education: "For in Calormen, story-telling (whether the stories are true or made up) is a thing you're taught" (35).

Stories can teach you lessons from different times and cultures that you might never have learned otherwise.

There are many things I have learned in Narnia that I would not have learned by simply growing up in America, but by learning them in Narnia I can try to practice them here. This is one of the main reasons why I encourage children to read the Narnia stories over and over again. They are not just fun to read; there are also many, many important things to be learned in them. If children do not grow up reading books like this, they are going to read (or, just as likely, watch) something else. Something else will fill the void—and it may not be the right sort of story at all.

So it is not enough just to be an avid reader. Eustace Scrubb was a reader when he was still in his nasty pre-conversion state:

> He liked books if they were books of information and had pictures of grain elevators or of fat foreign children doing exercises in model schools. (*Dawn Treader,* 3)

In short, the books he read were dull and boring and very modern and tiresome just like he was. Now Eustace, like many people, could convince himself that his reading was "useful" or "practical" for life. But information without soul, without a moral reference or worldview for understanding that information, is useless. Information is not at all a bad thing, but it is not a well-balanced diet for your mind and heart. It cannot inspire you to bravery, tune your emotions, or shape your character in any of the ways that a good story can. It is also important here to point out that the books Lewis describes here are almost certainly books about Joseph Stalin's Russia. Stalin died the year after *Dawn Treader* was published, and he was famous for putting up facades to take in gullible intellectuals from the West—in other words, people just like Eustace's parents. Books promoting communism and socialism as the future of society were thought to be very "progressive" in

Britain at this time, and Eustace's parents were clearly very progressive people.

So Eustace had read all the wrong kind of books, and his character was the worse for it. But it is accentuated when he arrives in Narnia. When Eustace gets lost on the dragon island, he sees an old dragon crawl out from a cave and die. He is petrified and has no idea what to do next. How does one deal with a dragon?

> [A]s I said before, Eustace had read only the wrong books. They had a lot to say about exports and imports and governments and drains, but they were weak on dragons. (87)

If he had read the right kind of story, he would know that dragons are well known for two things: hoarding treasure and telling lies. The latter is, in fact, part of the first story in Genesis: the dragon deceived our first mother in the garden, and greed (the lust of the eyes and flesh) was one of his tactics. Because Eustace doesn't understand that dragons cannot be trusted, he ends up sleeping on the dragon's hoard, thinking dragonish thoughts, and being transformed into a dragon himself.

## Loving Stories

I have talked a good deal about how stories teach us valuable lessons, but it would be a mistake to think that they are thus just the sugar coating that helps you swallow the bitter pill of each "lesson." Stories are not just vehicles for getting information into people's heads; they are something we can love for themselves.

When Peter, Susan, Edmund, and Lucy first meet Trumpkin, they are all impatient to hear his story.

"But it'll be a long story," said the Dwarf.
"All the better," said Lucy. "We love stories."
(*Prince Caspian*, 40)

The right kind of character loves the right kind of stories, and loving stories is a key part of being the right sort of character.

The love of story is extremely powerful because stories have a way of shaping what else we love. Stories build loyalties and allegiances; they divide; they tend to encourage the love of one thing and the hatred of another. We learn early on in *Prince Caspian* that Caspian is the right sort of character because of the stories that he loves. Even though he is a Telmarine, one of the race of people who basically committed genocide against the Old Narnians, how is it that we as readers like him and identify with him? Because he loves the stories of the "old things" which his nurse told him (41) and through those stories he gains a love for the old things themselves, as well as a hope for what the world should be: "like the stories" (47). The stories created in him all the right kinds of allegiances. Miraz, like most of the Telmarines, is immediately identified as the villain of the story because he hates the stories of Old Narnia. The Telmarines have a culture of guilt and fear about Old Narnia because of what their ancestors did to them. So they try to wipe out "even the memory of them" (51). Miraz gets very angry with Caspian (and his nurse) when he finds out that he has formed an attachment to these "fairy tales" (42). And at the end of the story Aslan makes an offer to the defeated Telmarines: live in peace with the Old Narnians or go back to the human world they originally came from. Why do many of the Telmarines decide to stay in Narnia? "Some of them, chiefly the young ones, had . . . heard stories" (214). Because they had heard the right kind of stories, they had formed the right kind of allegiances.

Occasionally, you will find a good character in Narnia who does not believe in the right kind of stories. I can think of only one instance, and that is Trumpkin. Trumpkin is a decent character who is loyal to Caspian, but he is a skeptic. He does not believe in Aslan or in the old stories about the four kings and queens of Narnia (Peter, Edmund, Lucy, and Susan). But it is important to note that he cannot stay that way. At some point he is confronted with the reality of the four children returning to Narnia, and later on he has to have an encounter with Aslan, who shakes him up and sets him straight. So Trumpkin is a rare exception to the rule. Almost always, knowledge of and loyalty to the right kind of stories is something that divides the good characters from the bad.

This theme comes up over and over and over again in the Narnia stories. Lewis is not just telling us a story, he's teaching us about stories in general, including his own story.

## Twisted Stories

Just as with authority, confession, nobility, and the other things we have talked about, stories can be twisted. Stories can tell lies. Stories can destroy lives instead of nourishing them, and stories can lead a person to form the wrong loves and loyalties. In *The Last Battle,* the centaur Roonwit gives the king this warning: "Sire, do not believe this tale. It cannot be. The stars never lie, but Men and Beasts do" (19). So stories can be conduits of both truth and lies. Stories in themselves are not automatically good; it has to be the right kind of story told by the right kind of person.

A good example is Nikabrik, who had more "faith" in the old stories than Trumpkin did. He says, "Trumpkin believed none of the stories. I was ready to put them to the trial" (166). But the fact that Nikabrik believes the old stories does not make him a good character, because he twists them the wrong way. He continues: "As for power, do not the stories say that the Witch defeated Aslan, and bound him, and killed him on that very stone which is over there, just beyond the light?" (168). He knows the story, and he believes the story, but he misses the point of the story entirely. He is willing for Aslan to have defeated the witch in the story, as long as Aslan will come and fight on Nikabrik's side against Miraz. But when Aslan does not immediately show up, Nikabrik is just as willing for the witch to have won in the story, as long as they can then call up the witch to help them fight Miraz. Nikabrik picks whatever elements out of the story that he wants to believe—whatever he can use to his own advantage in the present. When someone reminds him that Aslan came back to life and killed the witch, Nikabrik's reply still misses the point:

> "They say she [the White Witch], ruled for a hundred years. . . . There's power, if you like. There's something practical." (169)

The same kind of story-twisting happens all the time among modern historians and scholars who want to twist the historical record, or the classic stories, to serve their present agendas. They are not telling the stories honestly; they are merely trying to exploit them to gain power in the present.

In *The Last Battle* this kind of story-twisting is a key element. King Tirian and Jewel are trying to sort out all the terrible things that have been happening in Narnia and the rumors that Aslan is behind them. They know it does not fit with who Aslan is, because they know the stories about him, but they are also confused:

> "Is it not said in all the old stories that He is not a Tame Lion?"
> "Well said, well said, Jewel," cried the King. "Those are the very words: *not a tame lion*. It comes in many tales." (20)

> "Could it be true? *Could* he be felling the holy trees and murdering the Dryads?"
> "Unless the Dryads have all done something dreadfully wrong—" murmured Jewel.
> "But selling them to the Calormenes!" said the King. "Is it possible?"
> "I don't know," said Jewel miserably. "He's not a *tame* lion." (24–25)

They know from the old stories that Aslan is not supposed to be tame. But they also know that he is not evil, and the things going on around them, and being done in Aslan's name, are evil.

Shift twists the same line from the old stories to perpetuate his lies:

> "Aslan says he's been far too soft with you before, do you see? Well, he isn't going to be soft any more. He's going to lick you into shape this time. He'll teach you to think he's a tame lion!" (35)

Lying stories become all the more powerful when mixed with a bit of truth. When Puzzle is freed from Shift, thus endangering the whole deception, Shift then proclaims that a donkey with a lion skin has been roaming around pretending to be Aslan. So, "by mixing a little truth with it they had made their lie far stronger" (116). Stories are powerful things, and that is why the villains nearly always try to undermine them from within. It is far easier for bad guys to mix a true story in with their lies than to invent a new story from scratch, because by doing so they can take advantage of the power of true stories while twisting them to their own ends.

So far we have seen how stories tend to divide Narnians into two groups: the good characters respond to the true stories, while the bad characters hate the true stories and either try to deny them or twist them for evil purposes. But stories also help Lewis's characters discern which other characters are good or bad. In *The Lion, the Witch and the Wardrobe,* when all the children first enter Narnia together, they see a robin that appears to be inviting them to follow it. How do they know whether or not they can trust it? Edmund is suspicious:

> "We're following a guide we know nothing about. How do we know which side that bird in on? Why shouldn't it be leading us into a trap?"
>
> "That's a nasty idea [Peter replies]. Still—a robin, you know. They're good birds in all the stories I've ever read. I'm sure a robin wouldn't be on the wrong side." (61–62)

Peter is relying on what he knows from his reading to help make the decision on whether to trust the robin. If it was a vulture, he might have come to a different conclusion. Being steeped in the right kind of stories helps you identify good or bad characters when you meet them in real life.

Edmund, however, lacks this discernment. When he first meets the witch, she tells him,

> "If your sister has met one of the Fauns, she may have heard strange stories about me—nasty stories that might make her afraid to come to me. Fauns will say anything, you know." (40)

So we have two competing stories here—the witch's story and the faun's story. Whom to believe? If Edmund had learned anything from reading the right sort of books, he should know that the deathly white witch is not to be trusted. But he is deep in sin, and his heart is already half turned traitor. He does not recognize the story that he has found himself in, and he cannot discern the bad from the good. This much is obvious from the questions he raises later on when he is with his siblings again:

> "If it comes to that, which is the right side? How do we know that the Fauns are in the right and the Queen (yes, I know we've been *told* she's a witch) is in the wrong? We don't really know anything about either." (62)

Later on, what does Edmund say when they meet Mr. Beaver? "'I think it's a nice beaver,' said Lucy. 'Yes, but how do we *know?*' said Edmund" (65). And later, directly to Mr. Beaver: "'If it comes to talking about sides,' said Edmund, 'How do we know you're a friend?'" (67).

Edmund is trying to act like a "neutral observer." He apparently wants to conduct an independent, scientific investigation with lots of journalistic credibility and interview everybody involved, then make an intelligent, informed decision. He wants everyone else to consider the possibility that *both* sides could have valid perspectives. The problem is that he has no idea what story he is in, and he cannot identify the good characters or the bad. And what is worse, he has already given his allegiance to the witch by accepting her food and the enchantment that goes along with it. So although he pretends to be objective, he is anything but—it is just a lie he is telling himself to justify his own sinful actions. Edmund's example makes it clear that there are only two stories—Aslan's and the witch's. There is no third, neutral way. Beware the agenda of those who claim to have found it.

Edmund is already a traitor, but he distracts himself and others from that fact by questioning everyone else's trustworthiness. And he ends up twisting the story, just like Nikabrik:

> "Because," he said to himself, "All these people who say nasty things about her are her enemies and probably half of it isn't true." (89)

Even in this denial, it is clear that he knows the truth deep down. "*Probably*"? Edmund cannot even bring himself to say with certainty. "*Half* of it"? Even if half of what the good Narnians say about the witch were true, she would still be very, very wicked. Edmund knows it, but he chooses to tell himself a lying story anyway.

Digory gives us another example of how the stories we read help us identify the characters we meet. After Uncle Andrew performs an experiment on the unwitting Polly by sending her out of our world with a magic ring, Digory says to him,

> "I didn't believe in Magic till today. I see now it's real. Well if it is, I suppose all the old fairy tales are more or less true. And you're simply a wicked, cruel magician like the ones in the stories. Well I've never read a story in which people of that sort weren't paid out in the end, and I bet you will be. And serve you right." (27–28)

Digory has stumbled on his uncle's attic laboratory and discovered that magic is real. Well, if magic is real, Digory figures, then the stories he's read about magic are relevant here. Digory sizes up the situation right away because he has read the right books. He knows what story he has landed in, so he knows right away how to size up Uncle Andrew, who before this has been something of a mystery to him.

## The Real Story

In *The Voyage of the Dawn Treader,* Lucy is given the task of reading from a magician's book of spells in order to make the Dufflepuds visible again. As she is reading through the book, she happens upon something that is not a spell at all, but a story. It is the most beautiful story she has ever read, and she wishes it would keep going on and on. Eventually she comes to the ending, of course, and immediately she tries to turn the pages back and read it again. But she finds that she cannot; the book's pages only turn one way. And what is worse, she can no longer remember what the story was about, only how beautiful it was.

> And she never could remember; and ever since that day what Lucy means by a good story is a story which reminds her of the forgotten story in the Magician's Book. (157)

Even though she can no longer remember the story, now she really knows what a good story is like, and she uses it as the gold standard for good storytelling for the rest of her life.

Maybe you have had the same experience with dreams. Sometimes you will have a very vivid, beautiful dream, but when you wake up it is already half-forgotten by the time you sit up in bed. And by the time you walk across the room you cannot remember it at all. Only occasionally, much later, you will hear a tune or smell a scent that will bring back a hint of it.

The thing that keeps Lucy's experience from being tragic is that she does find that story again. In *The Last Battle*, when Lucy and the others enter into the final, glorified Narnia, they are entering into the fulfillment of all good stories—the real story that is truer than all the stories ever told before. Lewis writes,

> And as [Aslan] spoke He no longer looked to them like a lion; but the things that began to happen after that were so great and beautiful that I cannot write them. And for us this is the end of all the stories, and we can most truly say that they all lived happily ever after. (210)

He is saying that in one sense, the story has ended. He is not going to write any more books about Narnia. But his stories have ended because the real story has actually begun. All the best stories which had been told or lived out before this were like dreams compared to the real story that we will all eventually wake up into. That story is one that never ends, "in which every chapter is better than the one before" (211).

In other words, heaven is like a story, but one that is better than the best book you have ever read. The hints that Lucy got in the magician's book, or the hints that you get when you read a really great book or have an especially good dream—those all point to the final book. All earthly stories end, even when they are so good that you wish they would go on and on for thousands of pages more. But this final story will not end. Every chapter is richer, fuller, and more thrilling than the last. Eternal life is the ultimate story.

Every good story foretells this last one in some way. Every good story that is told here on earth has a kind of shadowy reality, but it always taps into a deeper reality and truth. J. R. R. Tolkien was once asked if he thought that *The Lord of the Rings* had actually happened somewhere, at some time. He replied, "One hopes." Lewis and Tolkien believed that storytelling was much more than just making something up. It was about human writers, as bearers of God's image, imitating God's work of creation. Even though they cannot create physical things in reality, they can still create worlds that resonate with the truth of God's reality. This is why Lewis said that a good adventure story is truer than a dull history. The events in the story might not have happened, but it more closely resembles the type of world that God made than a soulless retelling of true events. And when we finally enter heaven we will realize in full how all the best stories were prefiguring that last, greatest story of all.

# Conclusion

This is why it is so important for you to devote yourself to reading good stories. Life is too short for bad ones. Learn to read good stories and learn to write good stories too. Practice writing good stories by writing really bad ones, and by showing them to your teachers and parents and friends so they can help you make better stories. The Christian world needs far more good storytellers than it has.

Some of us might be tempted to think that the Christian world needs more theology books instead, but I think that is fundamentally against the spirit of the Bible. The Bible is not a book full of theology and doctrine. It is a book full of stories, poetry, prophecies, and songs, along with a few doctrinal books. Of course, I am not saying theology and doctrine are unimportant; they are essential. But most of God's word comes to us in the form of story. Whether they are the parables of Jesus or the great stories of the Old Testament, like David defeating Goliath, Jehoshaphat conquering with the choir in front of the army, the walls of Jericho falling down, the escape from Egypt and the dividing of the Red Sea—they all remind us to think about the Christian life and our relationship to God as a story. We are supposed to live like we are in one of God's stories.

This is why I believe that one of the most important things C. S. Lewis did for the Christian world was to bring back the centrality of storytelling. We do not need to feel guilty about loving these stories. We do not need to think, "If I were a *real* Christian I would be reading something more serious instead of these stories." Rather, we are *supposed* to love stories. We are supposed to think in these categories and try out these thought experiments. If you were with King Tirian in *The Last Battle,* what would you do? If you were sailing on the *Dawn Treader,* what kind of character would you be? How would you react in this or that situation? We are continually telling ourselves stories all day long. We convince ourselves that we are a certain kind of character and that our friends and family and other people we meet are other kinds of characters. What kind of story are you telling? Is it true?

I want to conclude with—what else?—a story. Over the years I read both the Narnia stories and *The Lord of the Rings* out loud many times to my children. Being impatient to do this, I started it much earlier than any normal person would, so that the first time I read *The Lord of the Rings* was when my son Nathan was two and my oldest daughter Bekah was four. At one point when I was reading one of the great battle scenes, my wife noticed that Nathan's cheeks had turned bright red, and when she felt them they were hot. He was two years old and he was *in* the battle. He was in the grip of the story. Now of course someone is going to say that when you read a book like that to two-year-olds, they are going to miss quite a bit. Of course they will. But that is fine, because they are going to read it again when they are six, and ten, and fifteen, and twenty. They are going to read it again and again, and they are going to get something more out of it each time.

The point is that human beings are wired to fall into the "story grip." God made us that way because it is a great way to learn. So learn from the story of Israel and from the parables of Jesus. Learn through the stories of great Christian writers like C. S. Lewis. Read them, reread them, and then read them again. When you let yourself be taken into these stories, you will not only enjoy them—you will be shaped and taught in many unexpected and useful ways, most of the time without even realizing it. That is the power of story.

# CHAPTER 6

# THOROUGH GRACE

NARNIA TAUGHT ME not only about Christ (through the type of Aslan) and the church (through the types of faithful Narnians) in and of themselves, but also about the nature of the relationship between Christ and His people. The best and simplest way of describing this relationship is that it is founded on *grace.*

Now grace involves much more than merely being "kind" or "nice." Grace means showing favor, giving, and bestowing. Because of the nature of the relationship between Creator and creature, all that we have and our very existence are completely and entirely *gift*—nothing else. If you give someone a Christmas or birthday present, they add it to all the other things which they own and which they got from any number of different sources. But when it comes to God's gifts to us, there is nothing we are or have which we did not receive from Him. This giving, this *grace,* is thus complete, total, and all-encompassing.

## Aslan's Sacrifice and the Foundation of Grace

The foundational story of grace in the Narnia stories is of course Aslan's sacrifice for Edmund in *The Lion, the*

*Witch and the Wardrobe.* But the two others that I learned most from are that of Eustace in *The Voyage of the Dawn Treader* and Jill in *The Silver Chair.*

As we consider the story of how Aslan redeemed Edmund in the first Narnia book that Lewis wrote, we need to remember that Aslan's death on behalf of Edmund was not just a specific act that saved him as an individual; it was a type or picture of what Aslan was doing for all of Narnia. King Tirian, in *The Last Battle*, describes Aslan as "the good Lion by whose blood all Narnia was saved" (40). There is another reference to this in *The Voyage of the Dawn Treader* when Edmund is talking to Eustace about how they both had been transformed by their encounters with Aslan, and Edmund mentions that he "saved me and saved Narnia" (111). So Lewis clearly wants us to view Edmund as the representative of all Narnians, all of whom need to be saved.

In the story of *The Lion, the Witch and the Wardrobe* itself, however, Lewis emphasizes Aslan's sacrifice for Edmund as an individual in order to illustrate the Christian doctrine of substitutionary atonement. Although this idea is central to the entire gospel message, sometimes it is difficult for us to understand it as an abstract doctrine. But when we read how Edmund betrays his siblings, how he is enslaved by the witch, how Aslan steps in and dies in his place, the nature of the exchange is clear. The witch was going to kill Edmund, but Aslan stepped in and offered himself instead. This is the foundation of the Christian faith—Christ died as a substitute for all His people.

But why did Aslan need to die? His mere arrival had already broken the witch's power and brought an end to her eternal winter. Edmund had already been rescued from the witch's grasp and brought safely back to the Narnians' camp. We might think that it should be time for the happy ending. But Lewis has a particular point to make: Even though Aslan had destroyed the power of winter, the witch still had a claim on Edmund's life because he was a traitor, and according to the law she had the right to have complete ownership of all traitors. The fact that Aslan had overcome her power and replaced winter with spring could not change that fact. Whose "law" was responsible for this? Remember that it is the law of the Emperor-Over-the-Sea, who represents God the Father just as Aslan represents Christ. Going against this law is out of the question. When Susan suggests it, Aslan is very displeased:

> "Work against the Emperor's Magic?" said Aslan, turning to her with something like a frown on his face. And nobody ever made that suggestion to him again. (142)

In other words, they can oppose the witch but they cannot oppose the witch's legitimate claim on Edmund, because to oppose that would be to oppose the Emperor Himself.

When Edmund realizes his situation, his reaction is telling:

> He felt a choking feeling and wondered if he ought to say something; but a moment later he felt that he was not expected to do anything except wait, and do what he was told. (143)

He has been brought to a position of complete helplessness. He can do nothing except wait passively for the outcome. He is not trying desperately to save himself or earn points that will somehow get him out of the situation. This is a picture of the sinner's situation before Christ saves him. Grace *happens* to you; it is not something that you can earn or "make happen" just by trying hard enough. Grace is something that you have to wait for. Now Edmund does not have to wait long; as you know, Aslan takes the witch aside and offers to give himself up instead.

Of all the things I have learned in Narnia, if I had to choose one single lesson that stands out as the most significant, it would be this lesson about the nature of substitutionary atonement. Even though I grew up in a Christian church and heard almost every Sunday that Jesus died for our sins, it was not until I read the story of Aslan and Edmund that the lesson really clicked. Suddenly I understood the cross—and the center of the gospel message—in a new and deeper way.

Lewis pays attention to the details in this part of the story by including many biblical allusions. For example, the Stone Table of course is the cross, and when Aslan dies it cracks down the middle, signifying that the power of death itself has been broken, while also echoing how the temple veil tore when Jesus died (Mt. 27:51).

The witch's attitude is also full of biblical allusions. When Aslan gives himself up to the witch, she thinks she has won. She thinks she has tricked him. She will get to kill Aslan, and then the next day her army will attack the Narnians and will get Edmund and all the others anyway. She thinks she has overcome Aslan, that his death will be utterly in vain, and that her reign over Narnia is intact. She thinks he is too weak and tenderhearted to make rational decisions. "'The fool!' she cried. 'The fool has come. Bind him fast'" (151). All of this alludes to what Paul says in 1 Corinthians 2:8: "Which none of the princes of this world knew: for had they known it, they would not have crucified the Lord of glory." Why would the rulers of this world not have crucified the Lord of glory? Because the very thing which they thought would give them victory turned out to be the instrument of their defeat.

We can find many other biblical allusions in the witch's treatment of Aslan immediately before his death. Since she has made her claim based upon the law of the Emperor-Over-the-Sea, you might think that she would simply perform the sacrifice quickly and get it over with. If it were merely a question of justice, you would think that the proceedings would be orderly and sober. But this is not what she does. She wants to torment him, mock him, and pour out all of her hatred on him before he is killed. She says, "Let him first be shaved" (153). This is what happened to Jesus also. As the prophet Isaiah foretold, he was tortured and mocked (Is. 53; Mt. 27:26–31). And like Jesus, Aslan does not resist: "But he never moved. And this seemed to enrage all that rabble" (154). Finally, as she is about to kill him, she heaps on one last word of abuse: "Understand that you have given me Narnia forever, you have lost your own life and you have not saved his. In that knowledge, despair and die" (155). Then, after Aslan is dead, she shouts to her followers, "It will not take us long to crush the human vermin and the traitors now that the great Fool, the great Cat, lies dead" (156). In other words, justice is not her intent at all. She is planning to break her part of the agreement by going after Edmund and the other Narnians as soon as she is finished with Aslan. She has merely used the claim of justice as a bargaining tool, and once she has achieved her goal she throws off all pretenses of pursuing justice.

But the witch has made a very profound mistake. At dawn, the Stone Table cracks in two and Aslan rises again. What does this mean?

"It means," said Aslan, "that though the Witch knew the Deep Magic, there is a magic deeper still which she did not know." (163)

The witch knows all about magic within time, but she knows nothing of the "deeper" magic from "before Time dawned." According to this eternal magic, "when a willing victim who had committed no treachery was killed in a traitor's stead, the Table would crack and Death itself would start working backward" (163). Notice that this deeper magic is from eternity. It is not rooted in the way of this world; it is rooted in God's ways. That is why the witch did not see it coming.

Through this story, Lewis manages to communicate what many theologians struggle to do: the substitutionary or "vicarious" death of Christ for His people. This is the meaning of the Christian faith—Christ died in your place, saving you by pure grace through no efforts of your own. In the same way, Aslan's central sacrifice is the foundation of all the grace that appears elsewhere in Narnia. And Lewis reveals the real nature of grace by having Edmund do absolutely nothing to deserve or earn what Aslan did for him.

# Grace Applied

### PART ONE: JILL AND *The Silver Chair*

Aslan's sacrifice for Edmund, and by extension the rest of Narnia, is the foundation of grace. But this grace still must be applied in the lives of specific individuals; it has to transform them. One very encouraging aspect of the Narnia stories is that the children who enter Narnia are all sinners. They all make mistakes. They all have real problems. They disobey, fight with each other, and even (in Edmund's case) betray their own family. They are not perfect by any means, which is why they need the transformative grace of Aslan. And it is important to note that this is true of both the "good" kids (like Peter, Lucy, and Jill) and the "record stinkers" (like Eustace). *All* need grace.

At the beginning of *The Silver Chair,* Jill is immediately a sympathetic character. Eustace, who has already been converted in *The Voyage of the Dawn Treader,* finds her crying behind the gym of their awful school because she has been bullied. When Eustace starts to talk to her about it, she flares up at him and brings up his past faults. He acknowledges those but reminds her how much he has changed, and she has to admit he is right. He then, hesitantly at first, tells her about Narnia and how it changed him. To his surprise she believes him and they decide to call upon Aslan together in the hope of getting back into Narnia, and Aslan grants their request.

They find themselves in Aslan's country at the utter East of Narnia, which Eustace and the others had reached at the end of *The Voyage of the Dawn Treader.* Soon they find themselves at the edge of a dizzying tall cliff and Eustace, who has no head for heights, starts getting weak at the knees. What is Jill's reaction? Heights do not happen to bother her, so "When she saw how very white he had turned, she despised him" (15). She steps right up to the edge of the cliff to show Eustace how much better she is. Now why does Lewis do this? He has already introduced Jill as a very decent sort of person who is mistreated by bullies. She has the reader's sympathy and is now on a grand adventure in another world, and yet this ugly side to her character immediately crops up. Lewis is reminding us that no one is free from sin—even those whom we think of as "good" people. Everyone is a sinner, and everyone needs grace.

So Jill looks down from the edge of the cliff to one-up Eustace, but she realizes that she has seriously underestimated this cliff. It is like no cliff that could possibly exist on earth; the tops of clouds are miles below and the bottom is nowhere to be seen. She finds herself succumbing to vertigo and losing her balance. Eustace, in a supreme act of bravery, jumps forward to save her; there is a brief struggle and Eustace ends up falling off the edge with a horrible scream. At this point a lion suddenly appears and with a great breath seems to blow Eustace off into the distance (to Narnia, as we later learn). He then walks away with no explanation, leaving Jill to ponder Eustace's fate and her own actions.

The accident happened because Jill despised Eustace and wanted to show off while taking him down a notch. She knows it, but she adds to her faults by not taking responsibility and trying to justify herself instead: "It's not my fault he fell over that cliff" (19). Note that the fact she keeps repeating this to herself is proof that it is a lie. If she really were innocent, she would not have to make a great effort to prove to herself that she is innocent. Jill may have escaped from her troubles back in England, but she has not escaped from the troubles in her own heart. She needs redemption.

In this condition, she suddenly notices that she is very thirsty and that she can hear the sound of running water in the distance. At length she finds a clear stream, but she stops short because a great lion is sitting between her and the stream—the same lion from the scene at the cliff. As readers, we know it is Aslan, but Jill does not. As she stands there deciding what to do, the lion invites her to drink from the stream. Now Jill is already very frightened, but when she realizes the lion is speaking, "It did not make her any less frightened than she had been before, but it made her frightened in rather a different way" (22). This is what Lewis elsewhere calls a *numinous* or supernatural fear mixed with awe. It is not the type of fear that you would feel from any physical danger, such as meeting an ordinary lion that escaped from the circus.

Now Jill is very thirsty, and it is clear that it is a spiritual as well as physical thirst. But her thirst has to contend with her fear of Aslan. Her resulting conversation with Aslan is one of the truly great passages in all the Narnia stories.

> "Are you not thirsty?" said the Lion.
>
> "I'm *dying* of thirst," said Jill.
>
> "Then drink," said the Lion.
>
> "May I—could I—would you mind going away while I do?" said Jill.
>
> The Lion answered this only by a look and a very low growl. . . .
>
> "Will you promise not to—do anything to me, if I do come?" said Jill.
>
> "I make no promise," said the Lion.
>
> Jill was so thirsty now that, without noticing it, she had come a step nearer.
>
> "*Do* you eat girls?" she said.
>
> "I have swallowed up girls and boys, women and men, kings and emperors, cities and realms," said the Lion. . . .
>
> "I daren't come and drink," said Jill.
>
> "Then you will die of thirst," said the Lion.
>
> "Oh, dear!" said Jill, coming another step nearer. "I suppose I must go and look for another stream then."
>
> "There is no other stream," said the Lion. (22–23)

This conversation is, first of all, a wonderful example of Aslan's refusal to negotiate with those who need his grace. You can imagine this conversation going quite differently with the modern evangelical version of Jesus in place of Aslan:

> "Oh, certainly I'll go away if you want me to. Let me know when you're comfortable with me coming back. . .

. No, no, no, I would never eat anyone. . . . You just wait until you're ready to drink. . . . Alright, well, I'm sorry you want to drink at a different stream. Good luck on your spiritual journey!"

Aslan is not like that. There is one way to life and that is through him, just as Christ says, "No man cometh unto the Father, but by Me" (Jn. 14:6).

There is more here as well. Jill's thirst can only be quenched by Aslan, but Aslan is also the one who gave her that thirst in the first place. Shortly after this, when Jill explains to Aslan that she got into Narnia by calling upon him, he replies, "You would not have called to me unless I had been calling to you" (24–25). Grace is a gift all the way down. God gives us grace, but he first gives us the desire for grace. As Paul writes in Corinthians,

> For who maketh thee to differ from another? and what hast thou that thou didst not receive? now if thou didst receive it, why dost thou glory, as if thou hadst not received it? (1 Cor. 4:7)

When Jesus comes to give each one of His people the gift of salvation, he extends the gift to you, and then His Holy Spirit awakens your desire for the gift and enables your hand to reach out and receive it. Salvation is all grace—all gift—from top to bottom and beginning to end.

## PART 2: EUSTACE AND
### *The Voyage of the Dawn Treader*

Eustace is probably the most well-developed character in all of the Narnia stories, aside from Aslan himself. Writers and critics often talk about characters being either "round" or "flat" according to how much time the author spends developing that character's personality. By that definition,

Eustace is a very round character. Lewis spends a great deal of time revealing his character, and several pages of the story are even written by Eustace in the form of journal entries that describe his first few weeks aboard the ship.

Through all this we learn a great deal about him in his unconverted state, as well as a detailed description of his conversion. Compared to Jill's experiences in *The Silver Chair*, Eustace's conversion in *The Voyage of the Dawn Treader* is much more stark. Jill starts out at least as a likable character and gradually learns how to follow Aslan faithfully, but Eustace starts out as the most unlikable character in the story and then experiences a rapid transformation.

It begins about halfway through the *Dawn Treader's* voyage. The ship and her crew have just endured some violent storms and finally reach a mountainous, heavily wooded island where they plan to stop, rest, and make repairs. Eustace, true to form, does not want to be put to work, so he wanders off into the interior of the island. After getting lost in the fog he finds himself in a remote valley, where he sees a dragon crawl out of its cave and abruptly die on the shore of a small lake. Just then, a great rainstorm rolls in, so Eustace takes refuge in the cave and ends up sleeping on the dragon's great pile of treasure. When he wakes up, Eustace realizes that he has turned into a dragon himself.

And after many days and weeks of living as a dragon, Eustace slowly begins to come to grips with his own character: "And poor Eustace realized more and more that since the first day he came on board he had been an unmitigated nuisance and that he was now a greater nuisance still" (104). His pride and blindness to his own faults are slowly replaced by an attitude of humility and repentance. He even starts to be helpful, lighting fires with his breath and carrying down to the beach a pine tree to serve as the ship's new mast. But—and this is very important to see—merely being sorry and trying to be good does not undragon him. He is a sorry dragon, and a somewhat helpful dragon, but he remains a dragon.

In short, Eustace still needs the grace of Aslan. So, as Caspian and the others are starting to discuss whether to continue on the journey and leave Eustace behind, Aslan appears to Eustace at night. Eustace's first reaction is the same kind of supernatural fear and awe that Jill experienced: "I wasn't afraid of it eating me, I was just afraid of *it*—if you can understand" (106–107). Aslan then takes him to a mountaintop garden with a deep well the size of a pool in the middle of it. When Eustace sees the pool, he immediately wants to bathe in it to soothe the pain in his arm—remember that when still a boy he had put a golden bracelet from the old dragon's hoard on his arm, and it has been digging into the flesh of his much larger dragon arm all this time.

But Aslan stops him from going into the pool, saying he must "undress" first. Eustace does not at first understand how a dragon could possibly undress, until he realizes that Aslan must mean that he needs to shed his scaly skin like a snake. So, he scratches and scrapes until a thin layer of skin comes off. It feels good, and he is just about to step down into the pool when he looks down and realizes that he looks just the same as before. So he peels off a second layer, then a third, but with the same result.

Eustace's attempts to scrape off his own dragon skin symbolize his efforts to repent and become a better person by his own power. He is trying to "undragon" himself. Like our own efforts to change our lives, it can feel good for a time. It can feel good to make resolutions about becoming a better person on your own. But all efforts to transform yourself with nothing but your own willpower are doomed to be superficial failures. It must be done for you. It must be done by grace, which means it must be a complete *gift*.

Eustace finally realizes this: "I just lay flat on my back and let him do it" (109). Aslan begins the work, as Eustace describes it, "Just as I thought I'd done it myself . . . only they hadn't hurt" (109). Eustace feels like Aslan's claws are going down into his very heart, and it is excruciatingly painful. Then Aslan throws his now skinless body into the pool. After this, the pain quickly vanishes and Eustace finds himself changed back into a boy. The entire scene is the picture of baptism and the "death" to the old, sinful self that the Apostle Paul writes about in Romans 6:1–4:

> What shall we say then? Shall we continue in sin that grace may abound? Certainly not! How shall we who died to sin live any longer in it? Or do you not know that as many of us as were baptized into Christ Jesus were baptized into His death? Therefore we were buried with Him through baptism into death, that just as Christ was raised from the dead by the glory of the Father, even so we also should walk in newness of life.

The other important lesson in *The Voyage of the Dawn Treader* passage is that when people try to be in charge of their own repentance, they can never go far enough. They never get past their own pain tolerance. You may remember falling down and scraping your knee when you were little, and your mother always wanting to clean the wound *very* thoroughly before bandaging it—she always made it hurt like crazy. She never let you do the cleaning yourself, because she knew that you would just gingerly dab around the edges and leave all the dirt and bits of gravel in the wound to fester later. It is the same way with repentance and grace—only God can deal with the root of the problem. God's way is much more painful, but it leads to a truly transformed life. Our way is much more comfortable in the short run, but it leads to agony and sorrow down the road.

Of course Eustace does not just change back into a boy and assume his past character again. His physical shape has changed, but so has his spirit. He has begun the Christian life, and he is now a boy in whom God is at work. This transformation, however, is not like flipping a switch. Eustace did not immediately become a completely different boy.

> To be strictly accurate, he began to be a different boy. He had relapses. There were still many days when he could be very tiresome. But most of those I shall not notice. The cure had begun. (112)

It is important to mention that God's work is a process. God does not change sinners immediately into sinless beings; he sets us on the path to sanctification that will occupy us for the rest of our lives.

# Conclusion

In these three "conversion" stories of Edmund, Jill, and Eustace, we see the foundational importance of Aslan's sacrifice and death. But we also see that when he died, those who follow him "died" also. That is what we see especially in the case of Eustace. And this reveals a very important point that we must make whenever we are talking about a substitutionary death—whether it is Aslan on the Stone Table in Narnia, or Jesus Christ on the cross in our world. There is a way of understanding substitution that is misleading. In a basketball game, if one player is substituted in for another, this means that the second player comes out. One man plays, and the other does not. Aslan did not die as a substitute in this sense, as we can see in our illustrations. The other kind of substitution occurs when we elect a congressman to go to Washington, D.C. and represent us. He is our substitute for us there, meaning that he represents us. When he votes, we vote. If Jesus were the first kind of substitute, that would mean that He died so that we wouldn't have to die. But He is the second kind of substitute. This means that when He died, all those who were represented by Him died also. And of course, when He came back from death, so did we.

The other foundational lesson in these stories is the "gift-ness" of grace. None of the three children could do anything to save themselves. In the end, they simply had to accept the sovereign grace that was given to them. Like God, Aslan does it all. The only thing we can do is accept it, and even our ability and desire to do that was given to us by God. Grace is *grace,* all the way down.

These things are the basics of the Christian faith. To learn them is to learn the gospel, but learning them in Narnia is a wonderful way to really *grasp* them on a level that no number of theology books or Sunday school classes can reach.

# CHAPTER 7

# ℒove for Aslan, ℒove for God

ONE OF THE great things about the Narnia stories is their very personal nature. All through the books, it is the person of Aslan that ties everything together. Loyalty to and love of Aslan characterizes all true Narnians, while a personal dislike of him characterizes those who are bad. Aslan is always the dividing line. Good and bad in Narnia are not determined by a list of abstract rules alone, but rather by *relationship*.

## Relationship to Aslan

There are many passages that illustrate this point, but here are just a few. In *The Last Battle,* how does King Tirian meet Aslan, when he finally makes it through the stable door to the final, true Narnia?

> Tirian turned last because he was afraid. There stood his heart's desire, huge and real, the golden Lion, Aslan himself. (167)

Tirian's deepest desire is not to be a generally good and decent person, or to serve the abstract brotherhood of mankind.

Aslan is his "heart's desire"; his whole life, and his destination after life, are directed by that personal relationship.

In *Prince Caspian,* when the four children are lost on their way to meet Caspian, how does Lucy know what path they ought to be taking? "'He—I—I just know,' said Lucy, 'by his face'" (126). Lucy cannot articulate how she knows what to do, but she is certain of it because of her personal knowledge of Aslan.

The same is true in many other passages. It always comes down to each character's relationship with Aslan and their personal response to him. Relationship and personality are commonly emphasized in our day, but unfortunately relationship is thought of as a universal goo—warm fuzzy feelings for all. But in Narnia, as in our world here, relationship is much sharper than that; relationship *separates.* Characters are good or bad by how they respond to Aslan and, in many cases, how they respond even to the *name* of Aslan. After simply hearing his name, some characters feel a flood of joy, while others get the creeps. This is one of the most important things that you can learn in Narnia, because the same thing is true in our world. We are all defined, most fundamentally, by our relationship to Jesus Christ. Many people want to pretend that this is not the case. They want good and evil to be defined in a much safer way, by conformity to rules and regulations—whether man's rules or God's rules, it doesn't matter—instead of by this relationship.

Your relationships determine whose side you are on. We have already discussed in the chapter on storytelling how Edmund attempts to posture as being the objective observer, but the passages are worth revisiting from the perspective of relationship as well. When Edmund is in the grip of the white witch, he is quick to raise questions when the others just seem to "know" that she is evil:

"If it comes to that, which is the right side? How do we
know that the Fauns are in the right and the Queen (yes,
I know we've been *told* she's a witch) is in the wrong?
We don't really know anything about either. "(62)

From a purely "scientific" perspective, Edmund could
have a point. These children have tumbled into this very
strange other world and they really do not know anything
about it. A short while later, he questions the intentions
of the robin and Mr. Beaver: "How do we know you're a
friend?" (67). Later, when Mr. Beaver mentions the name
of Aslan, Edmund feels a sense of dread and disgust, while
the others feel joy and hope. His hatred of Aslan and selfish loyalty to the witch are the core of his sin. Yet he is
unwilling to admit it. Deep down he knows he is on the
side of the witch. He has taken her food and her flattery,
and he is for all practical purposes her servant. But he
pretends that his relationship to the witch is not coloring
his perspective; instead, in front of the others he pretends
to be the neutral, objective, skeptical, and suspicious observer who demands rational proof of everyone's loyalties.
And that is a lesson we all need to file away in our minds:
Beware anyone who claims to be neutral, for they always
have an agenda.

Lewis uses this theme of personal affinities throughout
the Narnia stories. To take another example, we need go
no further than Eustace. Before he even gets into Narnia,
Eustace (and his mother) hate the picture of the Narnian
ship that is hanging on the wall of their spare bedroom,
while Lucy and Edmund are naturally drawn toward it.
After he, Lucy, and Edmund go through the picture into
Narnia, his natural loathing of all things Narnian continues. He hates the people, the monarchy, the ship, and
virtually everything else about it. After a while he makes
a very brief but revealing comment to himself as he lies

on the dragon's treasure: "With some of this stuff I could have quite a decent time here—perhaps in Calormen. It sounds the least phony of these countries" (87). So Eustace does not like anything about Narnia, but even with the little he knows about Calormen he instinctively feels that it is his kind of place—despite the fact that it is an oppressive and cruel empire. From the beginning, Eustace's character is revealed through his misplaced loves and loyalties.

Another example comes from *The Magician's Nephew*. Uncle Andrew has an instinctive hatred for Aslan's voice, even as Aslan is singing the glorious creation song that brings Narnia into existence.

> He was not liking the Voice. If he could have got away from it by creeping into a rat's hole, he would have done so. (108)

And why exactly did he not like Aslan's voice?

> And he had disliked the song very much. It made him think and feel things he did not want to think and feel. (136)

In those with sinful and stubborn hearts, the sight and voice of Aslan stirs up emotions that they do not want to feel—awe, guilt, fear, and more. Uncle Andrew did not want to feel these things, so he suppresses the voice of Aslan. He eventually convinces himself that the lion is merely roaring instead of singing or talking.

Jadis, the witch queen of Charn, has an even stronger reaction in proportion to her wickedness:

> But the Witch looked as if, in a way, she understood the music better than any of them. Her mouth was shut, her lips were pressed together, and her fists were clenched. Ever since the song began she had felt this whole world

was filled with a Magic different from hers and stronger. She hated it. She would have smashed that whole world, or all worlds, to pieces, if it would only stop the singing. (109)

I have already alluded to Edmund's first response to the name of Aslan in *The Lion, the Witch and the Wardrobe*. When the children are in the Beavers' house, Mr. Beaver tells them of the rumor that has been going around Narnia: "They say Aslan is on the move—perhaps he has already landed" (67). The other children feel a rush of happiness on hearing the name, but "Edmund felt a sensation of mysterious horror" (68). He shares this attitude with the white witch:

> "This is no thaw," said the dwarf, suddenly stopping. "This is Spring. What are we to do? Your winter has been destroyed, I tell you! This is Aslan's doing."
> "If either of you mentions that name again," said the Witch, "he shall instantly be killed." (122)

Edmund, Eustace, Uncle Andrew, and Jadis have this reaction in common, although on differing levels. Uncle Andrew is a less evil and more petty person than Jadis, and Edmund and Eustace (before their conversions) are even meaner and more petty—so their reactions are in proportion to their characters. But they all hate Aslan, his voice, and his works. They instinctively hate his goodness and holiness because they are not good or holy themselves. Jadis sums up this attitude nicely, speaking of the newly created Narnia: "This is a terrible world" (110).

This principle works in the other direction as well. While the bad characters instinctively love evil and hate goodness, the good characters instinctively hate evil and love goodness. When Polly, who is a very prudent and wise girl, jumps through one of the pools in the Wood Between the Worlds and finds herself in Charn, she knows exactly what kind of world it is right away: "'I don't like it,' said Polly with something like a shudder" (44). We have already seen how Uncle Andrew and Jadis heard Aslan's creation song later on in *The Magician's Nephew,* but now notice how the good-hearted cabbie has the proper reaction:

> "Gawd!" said the cabby, "Ain't it lovely?" . . .
> "Glory be!" said the cabby, "I'd ha' been a better man all my life if I'd known there were things like this." (107)

This same principle of separation based on one's personal reaction to Aslan is seen most clearly in the judgment scene at the end of *The Last Battle.* Aslan has called an end to Narnia, and all creatures come to the stable door where he waits:

> And at last, out of the shadow of the trees, racing up the hill for dear life, by thousands and by millions, came all kinds of creatures—Talking Beasts, Dwarfs, Satyrs, Fauns, Giants, Calormenes, men from Archenland, Monopods, and strange unearthly things from the remote islands or the unknown Western lands. And all these ran up to the doorway where Aslan stood. (174)

All through the Narnia stories, Lewis has provided various foreshadowings of how this principle of separation works, but they are all tiny pictures of the great separation on the day of judgment. In the end, everything comes down to a personal encounter with Aslan. The creatures do not recite what ideas or theologies they believe in; they simply look in his face and they either love him or hate him: "They all looked straight in his face, I don't think they had any choice about that" (175).

Lewis is showing us that judgment is not some bureaucratic or courtroom affair, with the stodgy inquisitor asking "What's your name?" and "What did you do with your life?" Rather, it comes down simply to whether you love and trust Jesus or not.

Those who look on Aslan with hatred, revulsion, and fear go one way:

> And when some looked, the expression of their faces changed terribly—it was fear and hatred. . . . And all the creatures who looked at Aslan in that way swerved to their right, his left, and disappeared into his huge black shadow, which (as you have heard) streamed away to the left of the doorway. The children never saw them again. I don't know what became of them. (175)

Meanwhile, those who look on him with love and joy enter into the new Narnia. And, it is important to remember that first appearances do not always predict the results of this encounter:

> There were some queer specimens among them. Eustace even recognized one of those very Dwarfs who had helped to shoot the Horses. But he had no time to wonder about that sort of thing (and anyway it was no business of his) for a great joy put everything else out of his head. (176)

The great judgment is important, but it is not the most important theme in this passage—that comes after the judgment: "'Further in and higher up!' cried Roonwit and thundered away in a gallop to the West" (176).

This "further in and higher up" is, on the surface, an invitation for the resurrected and glorified Narnians to explore the resurrected and glorified world of Narnia. On a deeper level, it is a metaphor for growing in the knowledge of Aslan. The more they learn about him, the bigger and more unexplored they find the subject to be. That is why when the Narnians follow this call and rush up the mountains, they find a garden at the top which turns out to be bigger than the whole world below, with yet more mountains in the distance—a larger and more real Narnia within the already glorified Narnia. The further in you go, the larger it gets. In the same way, the more we know and love God, the more we see to know and to love.

We can summarize this whole section in a few sentences. First, there are only two sides: that of God and that of His enemies. Accordingly, all people are now—and will be eternally—separated by their relationship to God. When you are out in the world and the question of which side you are on comes up, what will your answer be? The question should not be answered by some grand philosophical investigation; it should be answered by your loyalties and loves. Do you love God and His Son? Do you love His word? His people?

# Knowledge of Aslan

If knowing Aslan and being in right relationship to him is central, what then is it like to know him? Who is he? What kind of person is Aslan?

## TRIUNE AND INCARNATE

Shasta first converses with Aslan after he has completed his mission of delivering the warning to King Lune, but has become lost in the mountains. As he rides through the fog and darkness, He feels a great presence next to him, walking by his side.

> "Who are you?" he said, scarcely above a whisper.
>
> "One who has waited long for you to speak," said the Thing. . . .
>
> Once more he [Shasta] felt the warm breath of the Thing on his hand and face. (163)

This personal meeting with Aslan is very important for every character in the Narnia stories. Sooner or later, every main character must meet Aslan face to face. Whatever they are like before the meeting, and whatever mistakes or flaws they have, they are always fundamentally changed afterwards.

Now Shasta has met Aslan a few times before this, but he did not realize it at the time. First, a lion (seeming like a pair of lions) chased him and Aravis, bringing them together. Second, Aslan appeared as a stray cat that stayed with Shasta and comforted him during his ordeal in the tombs outside Tashbaan. And third, Aslan was the lion that chased him and Aravis during the final stage of their journey, giving them the last push they needed to complete their mission. So Shasta's adventure has been guided by Aslan all along, but Shasta still needs to have a personal meeting with Aslan, and it is this meeting which not only gives meaning to everything that has happened to him so far, but also changes him from that point onward.

So, how does Aslan finally reveal himself to Shasta?

> "Who *are* you?" asked Shasta.
>
> "Myself," said the Voice, very deep and low so that the earth shook: and again, "Myself," loud and clear and gay: and then the third time "Myself," whispered so softly you could hardly hear it, and yet it seemed to come from all round you as if the leaves rustled with it. (165)

This is a clear biblical reference to God, who told Moses, "I AM that I AM" (Exod. 3:14). The fact that Aslan repeats "Myself" three times in three different ways is also a reference to the Triune nature of God. Scripture conveys a similar point with one of the Hebrew words for God, *Elohim*. *Elohim* is the plural form of the word for "god," just as the Hebrew words *cherub* and *seraph* are singular but *cherubim* and *seraphim* are plural. So the confession of faith in Hebrew would be like saying "We believe in one Gods." The grammatical quirk conveys Trinitarian theology, and Lewis does a similar thing here with the threefold repetition of "Myself."

The effect of Aslan on Shasta is fear and awe mixed with joy: "A new and different sort of trembling came over him. Yet he felt glad too. . . . No one ever saw anything more terrible or beautiful" (165–166). Aslan is terrible and lovely at the same time, which is a fact that many Christians today struggle with. Some veer in one direction, emphasizing the loveliness of God without any of the terror, and they end up with a weak, sentimental goo-religion with no backbone. Others see only the terribleness of God, the hellfire and judgment, and tend to torture themselves and others with guilt, making everyone miserable and eventually driving people away from God altogether. Lewis reminds us that the beauty and terror are united and inseparable. God is the God of those who both fear and love Him.

Shasta's meeting with Aslan ends with Shasta recognizing Aslan's name, "Aslan, the great Lion, the son of the Emperor-over-the-sea, the King above all High Kings in Narnia" (166). Aslan then leaves him with a parting gift: in Aslan's footprint a spring of water has started bubbling up:

Shasta stooped and drank—a very long drink—and then dipped his face in and splashed his head. It was extremely cold, and clear as glass, and refreshed him very much. (167)

This fountain from the footprint is derived from medieval legends—remember that Lewis was a scholar of medieval history and literature—but it is also a biblical reference to "living water" given by Christ.

Aslan is a Person but also participates in a Trinitarian union; he is both beautiful and terrible; and his fundamental relationship to his people is that of life-giving grace. These are the key things Shasta learns. This meeting is also Shasta's *transformational* encounter with Aslan, although the transformation may not appear to be as sharp as Edmund's redemption or Eustace's "undragoning." But perhaps that is the point. Up until now, Shasta has been slowly changing and learning, a process that culminates in his courageous act of turning back to face the lion (which unknown to him, was also Aslan) chasing Aravis and Hwin. But the fact that he has endured hardships, acted bravely, and even accomplished his mission of warning Archenland is not enough. He must meet with Aslan personally, know him, and become his faithful servant. The transformation may not be externally dramatic, but it is no less real and no less necessary.

Another wonderful lesson from this same book is the *incarnational* nature of Aslan, which Lewis shows through Bree's first encounter with him. Remember that Bree is a Narnian horse who has spent most of his life as a Calormene warhorse. As a result, his knowledge of Aslan is rather muddled. When Aravis asks him why he always swears "by the Lion's Mane," he replies:

"All Narnians swear by *him*."

"But is he a lion?"

"No, no, of course not," said Bree in a rather shocked voice.

"All the stories about him in Tashbaan say he is," replied Aravis. "And if he isn't a lion why do you call him a lion?" . . . .

"No doubt . . . when they speak of him as a Lion they only mean he's as strong as a lion or (to our enemies, of course) as fierce as a lion. . . . It would be quite absurd to suppose he is a *real* lion. Indeed it would be disrespectful. If he was a lion he'd have to be a Beast just like the rest of us. Why!" (and here Bree began to laugh) "If he was a lion he'd have four paws, and a tail, and *Whiskers!*" (199–200)

(Just as he says this, of course, Aslan steals up behind him and tickles him with one of his whiskers.) In other words, before he is corrected Bree thinks just like a theological liberal. Christian liberals would like to deny that Jesus was really God, that he was born of a virgin, that he performed miracles, and that he literally rose from the dead. In the same way, Bree wants to spiritualize the stories about Aslan, because (he thinks) it would be just absurd and even *demeaning* to the true nature of God to take them literally. He wants to interpret them freely in order to get some nice-sounding life lessons and abstract truths, and then leave it at that.

But Aslan (like Christ) has a way of destroying such seemingly high-minded conceits. Aslan reveals himself to Bree, proving that he is an actual, literal lion with four paws, a tail, and whiskers. He tells Bree that his lofty-sounding thoughts were really not at all lofty enough: "Do not dare not to dare. . . . I am a true Beast" (201).

In the same way, Christ became a real man with a real body. This doctrine was shocking and offensive to the

Hebrews and Greeks, and it is still shocking and offensive to today's liberals. But nevertheless it is true. Jesus is not a myth or purely a symbolic figure or a theological concept. He is true Man and true God.

## SYMPATHY AND TENDERNESS

The fact that our God is a *surprising* God is one of the consistently helpful lessons that Lewis taught me through the character of Aslan. Some Christians who are overly "religious" in a fussy and tight-shoed way have false assumptions about God, and I appreciate the way that Aslan is constantly upending these assumptions in unexpected ways.

One of these surprising attributes of Aslan is his tenderness and sympathy toward his servants regardless of their many mistakes and flaws. In *The Magician's Nephew*, when Digory is worried about his mother's health, Aslan comforts him:

> "My son, my son," said Aslan. "I know. Grief is great. Only you and I in this land know that yet. Let us be good to one another." (154)

All through the book, Digory has been making mistakes. He rang the bell in Charn, twisting Polly's arm around her back in order to do it. He woke the witch, brought her back to London, and then into Narnia. Before Narnia was even an hour old, Digory had already brought evil into it. He is a young boy who has spoiled Aslan's creation, yet Aslan speaks to him like a son. He establishes common ground with Digory by pointing out the thing they share—grief. But perhaps Aslan's most surprising words here are "Let us be good to one another." Aslan is talking to Digory as a friend.

Many of us can imagine a brother, sister, parent, or friend talking like this and making this kind of close and sympathetic bond. But for some reason we do not often imagine God being in this type of relationship to us; we are tempted to assume (even if not in so many words) that God is too distant, too almighty, and too important to care about us individually in this way. But the Bible teaches that God does love and care about us in *exactly* this way. So if the thought of Jesus telling a sinful human being "Let us be good to one another" sounds disrespectful to you, then you have some things to unlearn.

Another example of this tender and individual relationship comes out of *Prince Caspian*. Near the end of the story, the Narnians are liberating the Telmarine towns and declaring the end of Miraz's rule. They suddenly happen upon Caspian's old nurse, who had been banished by Miraz years earlier for telling stories of the Old Narnia to Caspian when he was a boy. Her conversation with Aslan is brief but I think very significant:

> "I've been waiting for this all my life. Have you come to take me away?"
> "Yes, Dearest," said Aslan. "But not the long journey yet." (203)

Now the nurse is not at all a major character in the story. She is mentioned once at the beginning and again at the end. And yet Aslan calls her "Dearest." He has just as much of a personal relationship with her as he does with the main characters. In this brief moment Lewis gives us just a glimpse into this relationship to remind us that Aslan does not only care about the royalty or other important people in Narnia; he knows and cares for all of his servants individually.

Remember, though, that this tender love does not give a full picture of Aslan. As we saw previously in Shasta's encounter, Aslan is also powerful, exalted, and *terrible*. As Lewis writes in *The Lion, the Witch and the Wardrobe*:

> People who have not been in Narnia sometimes think that a thing cannot be good and terrible at the same time. If the children had ever thought so, they were cured of it now. (126)

There are many Christians who want to emphasize God's tender care above all else. They will talk about Jesus as if he were nothing but a friendly shoulder to cry on, a weak crybaby God who will suffer along with you and comfort you because he is too weak to do anything else. The full truth is far more wonderful and surprising than that.

After his resurrection, Aslan takes Lucy and Susan on a wild ride through Narnia to free those who were turned to stone at the White Witch's castle:

> It was such a romp as no one has ever had except in Narnia; and whether it was more like playing with a thunderstorm or playing with a kitten Lucy could never make up her mind. (164)

Aslan is also wild: "'He's wild, you know. Not like a *tame* lion'" (182), and he is certainly not safe:

> "Safe?" said Mr. Beaver; "don't you hear what Mrs. Beaver tells you? Who said anything about safe? 'Course he isn't safe. But he's good. He's the King, I tell you." (80)

Through the character of Aslan, Lewis wants us to realize that God is much, much bigger than any of our preconceptions. Too often we think we want a safe, tame God we can bring out of a box when we need some comfort, and then put back into the box so we can go on living our lives in our own way. But God is not what we expect or assume. He is good yet terrible, wild yet playful, tenderhearted yet quite unsafe.

## Worship and Imitation

The Bible tells us that when we look to Jesus, worship Him, and live in relationship with Him, then we become more and more like Him. The reverse is also true: those who worship idols become more and more like their idols (Ps. 115:8). In the same way, Aslan's servants become more like Aslan, while the Calormene culture that worships Tash becomes more harsh and cruel just like Tash.

One example of this is in *The Voyage of the Dawn Treader* when Lucy is on the island of the Dufflepuds. She is rummaging through the magician's book to find the spell to make the Dufflepuds visible again, but she stumbles upon a spell that would make her beautiful beyond all mortal reckoning. The pictures in the book even change so that she can see what she would look like with such beauty. This is a great temptation for her since she is the plain girl in the family; everyone considers Susan the attractive one. Fortunately, she just barely resists the temptation and avoids the disastrous consequences it would have had. But the result is that, by avoiding that sin, she later has the chance to find true beauty. When she finishes her task and turns around to find Aslan in the room:

> Then her face lit up till, for a moment (but of course she didn't know it), she looked almost as beautiful as that other Lucy in the picture. (158)

Lucy thinks about Aslan, is loyal to him, and obeys him; the result is that she reflects his beauty. She is made beautiful by beholding Beauty itself.

Later in the same story, the ship sails by the Dark Island, where dreams—including nightmares—come true. As they are trying to escape, things look pretty bleak until Lucy sees, flying around the ship, an albatross that "whispered to her, 'Courage, dear heart,' and the voice, she felt sure, was Aslan's, and with the voice a delicious smell breathed in her face" (187). Here, Lucy gains courage because Aslan is helping her to imitate him. Aslan was the model of courage when he sacrificed himself for Narnia, and he gives the same attribute to those who follow him and maintain a personal relationship with him. The same sort of thing happens to Lucy in *Prince Caspian*. She is encouraged and strengthened by him:

> She could feel lion-strength going into her. . . .
> "Now you are a lioness," said Aslan. "And now all Narnia will be renewed." (143)

In the same passage, Lucy also notices that Aslan seems to have grown, but it is only because she is imitating him:

> "Aslan," said Lucy, "You're bigger."
> "That is because you are older, little one," answered he. . . . "[E]very year you grow, you will find me bigger." (141)

This theme is also found in *The Last Battle,* as we saw that the further into the new Narnia they went, the bigger it became, and that this was a symbol of knowing Aslan. By following Aslan, the characters partake of his greatness and find that they themselves have grown greater in knowledge, character, spirit, and nobility. And the greater they become, the greater they perceive Aslan to be, and so on—in an upward spiral of growth.

Another example of this in *Prince Caspian* is when Aslan breathes on Edmund before he goes to deliver the challenge to Miraz: "Aslan had breathed on him at their meeting and a kind of greatness hung about him" (179).

And if Aslan can impart greatness, he can also impart humility. Just after Digory completes his quest to bring back the apple that will protect Narnia, Aslan commends him in front of all the creatures. But this does not puff up Digory with pride:

> [H]e was in no danger of feeling conceited for he didn't think about it at all now that he was face to face with Aslan. (*Magician's Nephew,* 180)

All these examples show how Aslan bestows his own attributes on those who follow him. As they worship and love him, they become like him. Aslan is strong and bestows strength. He is courageous and bestows courage. He is beautiful and bestows beauty.

Those who love Aslan want to be completely taken up and transformed by him; they want to imitate and become like him. In *The Horse and His Boy* there is a wonderful line, one of the best lines in all the Narnia stories. Hwin the horse, when she first meets Aslan, says to him, "I'd sooner be eaten by you than fed by anyone else." And Aslan replies, "Joy shall be yours" (201).

## Lies About Aslan

In the previous sections, we have seen the centrality of a personal relationship with Aslan. All creatures in Narnia are fundamentally divided into two groups: those who have and love this relationship and those who avoid it at all costs, thus entering into a relationship of enmity and judgment.

So relationship to Aslan is at the center of everything and is the defining characteristic of every creature's existence.

Now let's apply this one step further. If relationship to Aslan is at the root of everything, then ultimately all lies that creatures tell are ultimately lies about Aslan. This might at first seem like a big leap in reasoning; you might think, "Do you mean that if I tell a lie to my mother about whether I finished my homework or not, that I'm telling a lie about Jesus? That doesn't make sense. I lied about my homework, not about Jesus." Well, no, that's where you are wrong. If you understand Lewis's biblical vision, which is that all things exist in relationship to Aslan, then to tell a lie means that you are running away from the One who is the Truth. Every lie is an attempt to say that God is not God.

A great example of this truth is found in Shift's various lies about Aslan in *The Last Battle*. First, he uses his lies to gain a position of authority for himself, and then he uses that authority to fulfill his greed: "Now attend to me. I want—I mean Aslan wants—some more nuts" (33). But that is only the beginning. As he tries to extend his control over the Narnians, he twists Aslan's character into that of a hard taskmaster:

> "Aslan says he's been far too soft with you before, do you see? Well, he isn't going to be soft any more. He's going to lick you into shape this time. He'll teach you to think he's a tame lion! "(35)

Shift is steeped in lies. He tells lies to manipulate those around him in order to satisfy his greed for power and wealth, and Shift knows that lying about Aslan is the only way to really advance his prospects. All of his lies spring from the central lies that he has told himself about Aslan.

The last and worst lie is that Aslan and Tash are really one god:

> Tash is only another name for Aslan. All that old idea of us being right and the Calormenes wrong is silly. We know better now. (38)

Shift succeeds, for a time, in creating what many modern people would call "an advanced, liberal religion that blends the best from two great traditions of faith." Instead of Aslan *versus* Tash, he proclaims the name of "Tashlan." In the same way, we have many modern Shifts saying that Jesus and Allah and Buddha are really just different names for the same basic idea. The fact that the Calormenes sacrifice people on Tash's altar (37), while Aslan sacrifices himself for his people, is put aside as merely a minor disagreement. This is the lie of all lies.

## Through Aslan to Christ

I hope you can see by now that Lewis wanted relationship to Aslan and knowledge of Aslan to be at the very center of the Narnia stories. But it is important that we not miss the entire point and leave Aslan confined to Narnia—because Lewis wants us to learn about Aslan as he reveals himself in our world:

> "Are—are you there too, Sir?" said Edmund.
> "I am," said Aslan. "But there I have another name. You must learn to know me by that name. This was the very reason why you were brought to Narnia, that by knowing me here for a little, you may know me better there." (*The Voyage of the Dawn Treader,* 247)

And in *The Magician's Nephew,* remember how the cabby responded to the song of Aslan, and how later he responds to meeting Aslan himself:

> "Son," said Aslan to the Cabby, "I have known you long. Do you know me?"
> "Well, no sir," said the Cabby. "Leastways, not in an ordinary manner of speaking. Yet I feel somehow, if I may make so free, as 'ow we've met before." (148)

So the cabby lived as a Christian man back in England, which is why he recognized and loved Aslan in Narnia. Getting to know Aslan is like getting to know Christ in another way.

In other words, Lewis is not trying to lure children away from Christ by telling them stories about a lion. He is not setting them up for disappointment later in life. He does not want children to think, "Oh, wouldn't it be wonderful if Jesus were really more like Aslan! But we all know he isn't, so we might as well escape into Narnia and pretend that he is." That would be completely wrongheaded. Lewis takes us into Narnia in order to make us look differently at the world we actually live in. He wants us to realize that Jesus really *is* like Aslan. Instead of thinking about Jesus in the small, petty terms we sometimes fall into, we need to realize that Jesus is unsafe, just like Aslan. Jesus is good and terrible at the same time.

When you realize this, you can go back and read the New Testament from a completely new and fresh perspective, and you can start seeing—maybe for the first time—all the crazy things that Jesus said and did. We normally do not think that way. We think Jesus is the ultimate conservative, and all his followers should be prim and proper, never rocking the boat. It would be disrespectful, we are tempted to think, to describe Jesus otherwise. But, the fact is that Jesus Christ *did* say crazy things and *did* do crazy things. He said He was God, but He also had a physical body that needed food and sleep. He said the rich would have a tough time entering the kingdom of God. He told people to forgive each other instead of taking revenge. He went into the temple and, as I believe G. K. Chesterton once described it, "threw the temple furniture down the front steps." He did not behave himself. He was not a tame prophet. When we understand the character of Aslan, we are better able to understand Christ. And as we grow to love the character of Aslan, so we grow to better love Christ.

The whole point of introducing us to Aslan is so that we may come to a more mature understanding of Christ. This is why Aslan does not remain in his lion form at the end of the stories. In *The Last Battle,* after all is said and done, he reveals his true nature:

> And as He spoke He no longer looked to them like a lion; but the things that began to happen after that were so great and beautiful that I cannot write them. And for us this is the end of all the stories, and we can most truly say that they all lived happily ever after. (210)

So, Aslan eventually manifests himself in his full character as the Lord Jesus. Now of course the symbolism does break down a bit here, and there are some wrinkles that might need to be worked out, since previously Aslan had described himself as a "true Beast." The lion form is not a mere appearance; he is not just Narnia's God in a lion suit, no more than Christ is God in a man suit—the creed says that Christ is *true man.* But the one thing we can be sure of is that Aslan's true form was not a kind of spiritual or ghostly being. Rather, the whole context of this passage invites us to think of these heavenly realities—including the resurrected body of Christ—as *more* solid and tangible than the "real life" that came before. In another of Lewis's books, *The Great Divorce,* he describes heaven as a place of real solidity and real color compared to the shadowy ghost world down below. We sometimes think that when Jesus rose from the dead, He turned into a kind of ghost. After all, didn't He walk through the walls of the upper room where the disciples were meeting? The problem is that it never occurs to us that the *wall* was the ghost. Jesus could walk through the wall because He is more solid and more real than the wall. So when Lewis describes Aslan changing his form at the end of *The Last Battle,* he is encouraging us *not* to think of this form as a sort of ghost-Jesus body, but rather the true, ultimate, solid, bodily reality of Christ.

# Conclusion

Philosophers have for a long time tried to make ethics—the study of right and wrong—into a very abstract intellectual exercise. They have tried (and failed) to show how to arrive at definitions of good and bad based purely on their reason. Lewis shows us a different way. You know right from wrong, good from evil, and wise from foolish based on the basic relationships and loyalties in your life. The primary relationship is with Jesus Christ, and the secondary relationships are to your parents, teachers, and pastor.

When you truly love God and seek to behave always in the light of your relationship to Him, obedience becomes instinctive. You do not have to haul out a rulebook and thumb through it to figure out what rules you should be obeying in this or that situation. Instead, it is a matter of pleasing God. Sometimes, in the complexity and messiness of real life, it can be difficult to sort out what you should do. In this case, your mental rulebook can easily fail. You may never have encountered a situation quite like it before, and thus you don't know what rules to follow. But instead of asking about rules, ask yourself, "What choice here would make Jesus happy? What would make my father or mother happy?" And, for those of us who grew up with the world of Narnia, we could ask ourselves, "What would make Aslan happy? Is this the sort of behavior he would approve of, or is it the sort of behavior that would cause him to make a low growl?"

This is how we should measure everything: in terms of personal relationship. Living in Narnia for a while can help you build that relationship in many ways. Knowledge of Aslan brings you to better knowledge of God; love for Aslan brings you to better love for God.